Elegy of the Minotaur

by

Barak A. Bassman

TELEMACHUS PRESS

Cover designed by Telemachus Press, LLC

Cover art:
Copyright © iStockphoto/35277232_illustra_Crowoman

Published by Telemachus Press, LLC
http://www.telemachuspress.com

ISBN: 978-1-942899-66-2 (eBook)
ISBN: 978-1-942899-67-9 (Paperback)
ISBN: 978-1-942899-68-6 (hardback)

Library of Congress Control Number: 2015957772

Version 2015.11.27

10 9 8 7 6 5 4 3 2 1

Elegy of the Minotaur

I. The Birth of a Monster

QUEEN PASIPHAE OF Crete, who was formerly so light on her feet, was suffering horribly from her unexpected pregnancy. Her belly swelled beyond all normal human proportions. Her belly, in fact, was soon so massive that she was bedridden. Her feet swelled painfully; her shoes could not fit on her feet, and she was forced to waddle uneasily when she tried to walk, usually holding the hand of a nearby servant to help balance her new girth. Her hands swelled too, and she could not move her fingers easily. She could not hold a glass or food, and she had no choice but to be fed by her servants. In sum, the queen was rendered helpless by the growing life inside her, which had somehow taken control of her once tightly poised, lithe body.

There were no more garden strolls with her friends under the dazzling bright Mediterranean sun. Now Queen Pasiphae was pinned to her bed in her tower, staring every day at the same picture on the wall of a satyr playing the flute for an adoring group of sea nymphs as the beach's waves foamed and the moon looked down kindly. The queen had once considered this picture to be so charming, and after a night of dancing and drinking, she would gaze at it as she fell asleep. Now the picture seemed to taunt her cruelly, with its promise of beaches and swimming and bodies that could still move easily. These bodies did not know or care how lucky they were in their mobility. The bedridden woman felt she had little to look forward to besides ringing her bell and demanding to be fed whatever bizarre new food combinations were insisted upon by the unruly new tenant in her abdomen:

fish and honey, olives and grapes, the endless culinary creativity of the invader who had seized and deformed her once beautiful body.

At one point, Queen Pasiphae begged a midwife for a special potion to end the pregnancy. The good midwife complied. One night, discreetly, the midwife slipped into the queen's bedroom with a small vial of white, thick liquid. It smelled of soap, but Pasiphae forced herself to drink it. The midwife assured her that by morning it would all be over; a small fit of bleeding, a day or two to recover her strength, and she would be walking again, with her hands and feet deflated to their normal size. The queen fell asleep with a smile on her face. She looked at the frolicking sea nymphs and thought she would soon join them on the beach.

The midwife returned the next day. She strode into the bedroom with wide, confident steps, certain she had conquered her mistress's monstrously large fetus. She was grinning with excitement. There was the queen, however, just as she had been: as swollen as ever, buried under her great belly, which seemed, if anything, even larger. But now the queen's face was drained of all color. She was sneezing repeatedly. With each sneeze her bloated body shook and rattled futilely under the great swollen womb.

Have you started bleeding yet? the midwife asked, her voice cracking at the question's end. The midwife moved towards the bed and her eyes scanned the sheets for some telltale sign of blood. Her eyes darted around quickly, again and again over the same few patches of nightgown, sheet, and floor. The midwife's eyes could not find what they were looking for.

Nothing happened, replied Queen Pasiphae. I feel so ill, so terribly ill. Another sneezing fit followed. The sneezes were so loud that the midwife jumped back. The queen's body vibrated in pulsating waves with each new sneeze. The midwife looked at her feet. She shifted her weight from one foot to the other. Her fingers quickly joined and then separated several times.

Still looking down, the midwife said in a whisper, I am sorry, Great Queen, but the potion has always worked before. There is something different about this baby. I am so very sorry.

The queen said nothing. She turned her head away from the picture of the sea nymphs and towards her window. The Sun shined through the window into the room. The window was framed by simple beige stones. The blankness of the stones was a comfort.

The midwife shuffled out without speaking further or raising her head. The queen's smile had faded into a grimace of resignation. Her eyes were empty of feeling. She did not try to move anymore under her overbearing weight; she merely stared at the beige stones.

The months were excruciating for Queen Pasiphae. She was certain that her beautiful slender figure was being ruined forever. Maybe that would satisfy her husband, King Minos. No men would now line up to caress her fat, swollen body. She drifted between pain and fitful sleep.

At last the labor pains came. Queen Pasiphae's screams could be heard across all of the city of Knossos and probably across the island of Crete as well. There was a veritable army of midwives and physicians around her bed attending her. She had never felt such horrible, horrible never-ending pain. Her body convulsed over and over again; she wanted it to stop, but her mad womb had a malicious will of its own and would not relent. Indifferent to Pasiphae's wishes, her body violently contracted its muscles. She sweated terribly and screamed about wild visions of great white bulls running in pastures and blessing the world with their gentle ways. Sometimes she screamed remorseful laments about how she had sinned against the gods and begged their forgiveness. The midwives were used to the angry and delusional sobs and rants of their patients in labor and paid these words little mind; they just told her to breathe slowly and that soon she would cradle a beautiful small child.

The midwives' rote reassuring words turned out to be lies, and there was worse horror coming for Queen Pasiphae. The chief midwife saw it first. She saw the baby's head crown from between Pasiphae's legs. She gave a clap of joy. I see him coming, almost done, almost there. Your beautiful baby is ready to come into this world, everything will be better when his tiny hand wraps around your finger.

The midwife continued. He will be a big boy, already with a thick, fine head of hair. Yet soon the encouraging words died down without any explanation given to the heaving, sweating mother to be. The midwives and physicians crowded around Queen Pasiphae's open legs. They were deathly quiet. Pairs of eyes glanced quickly down and from one person to another.

The helpers became stiff and immobile, except for their rapidly darting, almost manic, eyes. There were no longer any sounds but Pasiphae's cries of pain.

Out the baby burst from Queen Pasiphae's womb and gave a good loud cry. He flew forward, still tethered to the umbilical cord, and landed on a nearby midwife who instinctively caught him. She was surprised at the heavy weight. A big one, she thought; so this was the great big baby that had crippled his mother for so long.

The midwife looked down. She shuddered. She looked up. All eyes, except Pasiphae's, were gazing at her and the strange baby. She looked about holding the baby outstretched to see if anyone would take him from her. No one moved to help. The midwife grabbed a blanket, swaddled the baby with a few sure, well-practiced movements of her hands, and put him in the cradle that had been left near the bed in anticipation of the forth-coming birth. She stepped back, slowly, walking backwards and not taking her eyes off the newborn swaddled bundle.

Queen Pasiphae demanded to see her baby. She wanted to see her promised reward for the months of agony and the terrible pains of labor. No one moved to pick up the child. Queen Pasiphae became upset, and she berated the midwives. She demanded her child. She would brook no more delay. After another pause where many fingers fidgeted and panicky eyes sought to escape both mother and child, one midwife picked up the child wrapped in the warm blanket and handed him to the new mother.

There he was: from the neck down a newborn baby boy like any other, except bigger, but not too much so. However, from the neck up, the queen found a baby bull with a calf's head and big sad, sweet eyes. Queen Pasiphae held him to her breast and announced to the silent crowd, who continued to look away from her, that she thought her newborn baby son was beautiful and looked just like his father. This statement was followed by more silence. The bodies in the crowd twisted and swayed awkwardly, with jerking, restless motions, although they all stayed in place. Queen Pasiphae looked at them all and she felt angry. She dismissed everyone except one midwife to assist her with the baby.

King Minos, the queen's husband, was, of course, informed at once of the birth of the unusual new royal prince. He refused to believe the news, but could not figure out why he was being deceived and in such a bizarre manner. He went to his wife's bed chamber to congratulate her and to discuss public ceremonies appropriate to the occasion of the birth of the royal heir.

King Minos walked slowly but with assurance into the queen's room. His gait was swift and firm and he had a slight but reserved smile—festive, but measured. Upon entering the bedroom, King Minos saw a little baby in a blanket with a calf's head sticking out and suckling his mother's breast. His firm stride abruptly halted and the smile vanished. He looked between mother and baby monster several times. He dismissed everyone else in the room.

How did you birth a monster? This cannot be my son. What have you done? What terrible crimes have you committed to be punished so hideously?

Queen Pasiphae was calm. She looked her husband straight in his eyes. Her voice was even but firm: He is no monster, he is beautiful, he is mine. I had a lover who was greater than any man, but I can never see him again. This was his parting gift to me.

The King staggered out. He was not sure which, if any, part of his wife's mad tale to believe. He sent for his soothsayers: What did this omen mean? What should be done with the baby monster?

The soothsayers pondered and consulted the signs of different omens, but reached conflicting opinions:

This was a monster, a portent of doom that should be exposed in the wilderness and left to die.

This child was a sign of strength. Crete was strong as a bull and would have a new Heracles, part man and part bull, to rule it. This child was no doubt a gift of the gods, perhaps even the child of one of the gods.

The child was bewitched. An evil witch, in the employ of the King's enemies, had cursed the young prince and sacrifices must be made to the gods to appease them and to persuade them to restore the child's true human form.

None of these contradictory words reassured the king, much less gave him the guidance he needed in the midst of his reeling confusion. He scowled and said nothing to the soothsayers. Nevertheless, King Minos knew that news of the monster child would be spread by the many servants and physicians and midwives and conjurers who had now all seen him. The king needed an explanation for his lords and his subjects. He mulled the situation further and then summoned the chief priest of Poseidon's temple in Knossos. The two spoke, alone, for a long time.

King Minos let four days pass without making any comment on the baby monster. During this time, he made no effort to halt the spread of rumors throughout the palace and the capital city of Knossos. He was often seen pacing his rooms and hallways, restless and sleepless. Sometimes he would snap angrily at someone who passed by and berate the poor soul for not doing his or her duty correctly, no matter how trivial. Every tray of food was carried in the wrong way in those tense days in the palace. He canceled all his appointments and shut the palace gates to visitors. The king was soon left alone by his retainers who chose to put off their business for another more suitable time.

After these four days of brooding, King Minos led a deliberately public, ornate procession to the temple of Poseidon. Queen Pasiphae walked next to him, holding her baby monster. The king's bearing was erect, his step slow and calculated, and his eyes faced forward. He never looked at the queen or her strangely large, swaddled baby monster. The queen gazed dreamily at her newborn baby monster as she went and was oblivious to the crowds watching her as many among them wondered what great sin she had committed against the gods. She reached her finger into his palm and smiled warmly as he reflexively wrapped his hand around it.

The king had directed that all his lords, ministers, and soothsayers were to follow him in a long, synchronized line, flanked by heavily armed and grim soldiers. The group marched in somber lockstep with heads staring at the ground. They were silent, mostly. There was an occasional rapidly whispered word in a worried tone; but no words were spoken aloud, and certainly no such words were meant to reach the ears of the king or queen. Crowds swarmed around the procession, and foreign ambassadors discreetly watched from a distance, carefully observing the spectacle and jotting down notes for the next dispatch to their home courts.

King Minos reached the temple first and prostrated himself before a statue of Poseidon. He beseeched the god for guidance on how to treat his deformed, monstrous son. The chief priest, who was at the altar nearby, walked over to Minos and announced that he had received a vision from the great god, Poseidon:

In a dream last night, the priest recounted, Poseidon came to me. He was wearing a blue cloak and carrying his Earth-shaking trident. Poseidon told me that you, King Minos, would come to see him today to pay obeisance. Poseidon gave me the following message for you: I, Poseidon, lord of the sea and shaker of the Earth, gave you, King Minos, a great white bull as a pledge of my loyalty to you. After you vanquished your foes, you were supposed to sacrifice that bull to me, for it is I who has made you great. But instead, you were greedy and defiant and wanted to keep the bull and its precious meat for your own belly. Thus, I cursed Queen Pasiphae with a desperate love for the bull. She had craftsmen create a disguise in order to appear as a cow to the bull so she could lay with him. The result of Pasiphae's hideous sin is the monstrous child she now suckles.

To atone for your sin, you must sacrifice the great white bull without delay. However, you are not to harm the child. He is my child. Should you harm the child, I will shake the ground upon which you walk and bring your fine Knossos crashing down into rubble, and I will send great waves to wreck your harbors and fleet of ships.

King Minos fell to the ground and prostrated himself before the altar. He shed copious tears and begged for the god's mercy. Three lords grabbed the nearest horses and rode back to the palace to fetch the white bull for immediate sacrifice. They were followed by a great and eager mob.

Queen Pasiphae felt sad that the white bull would be killed. When she saw him dragged up to the altar, she looked intensely into his bovine eyes. She was sure that he returned her passionate gaze, if just for a moment, and then hung his head down as he was led to his doom. She wondered if that downward swing of his head was a mark of noble, brave resignation or of bitter shame. She clutched her baby monster tightly as the priestly knife swiftly slashed the bull's throat. The white bull fell limply, but without any scream of protest. He died a tranquil philosopher's death. Pasiphae wished his soul a good journey to Hades, although she reflected that she did not know exactly where the souls of dead animals went after death. She did feel, though, that this great white bull had a generous soul, which he had shared with her in happier days, and he deserved to be rewarded for the upright life he had led.

Queen Pasiphae was amused by the priest's tale, although she carefully wiped away the smirk she felt spreading across her face during his performance for the crowd. This was a solemn occasion and it would not do for the queen, who was already being publicly shamed, to appear to sneer arrogantly at the god's chastisement. But she knew the story he had spun of the baby monster's origins was only partly true. Queen Pasiphae was the daughter of one of the great landowners of Crete and had been able to offer a great dowry to a worthy future husband. Her wealth and easy graceful beauty, long and willowy and pale, with messy, light chestnut curls, made her the natural match for the ambitious, young Prince Minos. The marriage sealed important alliances between the royal family and the magnates of the countryside. Minos had plans for costly foreign wars, and he needed to secure the domestic peace.

King Minos proved to be a hard husband for the young bride. He was often away on military campaigns on the Greek mainland, subduing one city or another or enforcing Crete's ever escalating demands for tribute against smaller states. His great joy was to march with an army, sleep in a makeshift camp, and lay waste to his enemies' lands and, more often than not, plenty of their inhabitants, too. He had little interest in spending time with his wife, whose humdrum, palace-bound concerns bored him. She would speak to him of banquets, music, theater, new paintings, the royal gardens, and he did not even know or care what else. He would look at her eyes in an expression of strained attention, but soon her words dissolved into a hum of unintelligible sounds tossed from her lips at his head, while his mind drifted to his next campaign and wandered feverishly across imaginary military maps.

Queen Pasiphae naturally became lonely. She sought out lively and frivolous company to distract her from her cold, distant husband and his relentless focus on shedding blood. She gathered a circle around her, of young noblemen and women, who enjoyed music and theater. They would stage amateur performances together, usually comedy. The men were drawn to Pasiphae's beauty and teasing smiles. They would sprinkle their conversations with a steady stream of compliments whose seriousness was cloaked in sarcastic tones and mock heroic deeds of securing wine or cheese or a garland of flowers. Pasiphae never encouraged them, at least not too much, and she loved hearing their words. She would blush and scold them playfully, warning that this was no way to act with a married lady.

Tales of these innocent games, conveyed with malicious insinuations, reached King Minos. He boiled with rage. He was convinced that his wife was betraying him while he protected Crete's interests abroad. One of these noblemen no doubt was using her and had designs on the throne. King Minos had these men followed and watched.

Once he was told that a young man in a play with Pasiphae had dared to kiss her in a scene where the dashing young prince—that was he, the young man—had finally saved the princess—that was Pasiphae—from a power-hungry mouse that had eaten all of her sweets at night. King Minos ordered his guards to seize the man from his bed that night, take him outside of Knossos, and return him to his country estate. In addition, they were to warn him never to set foot in the palace again.

When the Queen learned of her good friend's banishment, she strode forcefully into the king's bedchamber. She demanded that her friend be returned to the palace at once. The king had no business threatening her friends. This was an outrage. She would not stand for it.

The king slowly raised his head. He breathed hard; he was visibly containing himself. In a monotone, hard voice he held his ground: The queen's conduct must be above reproach, especially because he had devoted himself to subduing Crete's enemies and safeguarding the island kingdom through military campaigns, which necessitated long absences from the palace. She was shaming him by her indiscreet behavior. She needed to start behaving with dignity.

The queen's body tensed. Her eyes stared straight into her husband's. She demanded again the return of her friend. She would not leave, she said, until the king revoked his unjust decree. She crossed her arms. Her glare did not waver.

The king was silent. He stared at her curiously; he seemed surprised by her stubbornness. He waited. She held her ground. He tapped his feet, fiddled with dispatches from his generals, and was soon pacing the room.

King Minos put all his energy into avoiding his wife while he play-acted at being the busy and plotting monarch.

Queen Pasiphae kept her eyes fixed on her husband.

The king stormed about the room, picking up now this letter or examining that dagger. He hopped from task to task to task. Finally, he looked at her. The same glare was still boring into him. He made a signal with his hand. Two guards walked over. Each one grabbed one of the queen's arms. They led her out of the room and back to her suite of apartments. At first she protested, but soon gave up.

King Minos's cruel sense of humor led him to a fateful revenge on Queen Pasiphae's perceived betrayal. After Minos drove away her friends, one by one, the queen complained constantly about her loneliness and boredom. So Minos dreamed up a dreadful job for Pasiphae: she was to monitor the royal animal stables. This was a task that the king and all of his ministers loathed: the cramped wooden stables, with their stifling air stinking of animal sweat and manure and hay. They despised the darkness of the stables, no windows, only openings in the wooden walls, small and slanted, letting in barely any light. The place was a putrid, dank underworld.

Worst of all was the steward in charge of the stables. This man had been born a palace slave, assigned to work in the stables as a boy. By early manhood he had become the steward of the royal herds and flocks. Now an old man, gray, bent, mostly toothless, stinking of the same foul odors as his animals and stables, he spoke endlessly of the animals under his care. As he never married and had no living relations, these were his only family. He shared every detail of each animal's daily life with anyone foolish enough to visit his domain: what it ate at each meal and how much, the amount and frequency of its urine and bowel movements, and the odor and color of each, all meticulously tracked. He even detailed their illnesses and warts and blemishes. He would become so engrossed in these lectures that he never noticed his audience's thoughts wander to prettier subject matter.

Twice a week, after breakfast, Queen Pasiphae was escorted by her guard to the stables, where she met the steward. As even the guards could not tolerate the stench and the incessant chatter of the man, the queen was left alone with him to tour the stables and inspect the animals. This should have been a quick job. The steward, however, starved of company and overjoyed at what he assumed was a sympathetic ear, launched with gusto into excited speeches about each animal. These speeches were often difficult to understand because the old man had almost no teeth left, and thus, he spoke by spitting his words out of his throat, trailed by strong gusts of his moldy breath. No animal could be passed without a discussion of its parents and its life so far; a detailed explanation of its diet both today and in the past, with learned asides as to why subtle shifts had occurred. He often gave a full medical history and, of course, an exact recitation of the number, color, and smell of each animal's urine and manure, accompanied sometimes by the steward scooping up a sample to show the queen, so as to demonstrate the soundness of his observations. This whole tour took almost an entire day. Compounding the misery of this ordeal, the steward, old and gaunt, his body fading away further with each passing year, had no need of food and drink and, therefore, the queen ate and drank nothing between breakfast and a late dinner. The thirst was especially difficult: sweating liberally in the dark, hot, moist stables, the queen found it difficult to keep standing without water or wine.

Making matters still worse, the old steward had a terrible memory. As a result, he never recalled what he had said during the last tour and inspection, and thus repeated himself, in full, each time. There were, in fact, few, if any, developments to report from visit to visit. So Queen Pasiphae was forced to endure the same lengthy recitation of the same epic song about animal husbandry on each tour.

At first, the queen loathed her duties in the stables. After the first tour and inspection, faint from lack of food and drink, nauseated by the putrid smells, and her head throbbing from the drone of the old steward's pounding babble, Pasiphae stormed into a meeting of King Minos and his generals. She warned the guards off. The guards stepped back while looking at the king, but he nodded his assent.

Queen Pasiphae reminded her noble husband, the King, that she was Queen of Crete and entitled to the dignity of a great queen. She had been raised as a Lord's daughter and had learned to weave and sing and write elegant letters. It was not her place to roll around with pigs and horses. This was disgusting and demeaning and an unforgiveable insult to her. She would have no compunction about leaving the palace and demanding the return of her dowry.

King Minos sat stony-faced through this speech. With a wisp of a grin on his lips, he calmly replied that he indeed recognized her great lineage, fine upbringing, and incomparable beauty. It was because he esteemed her talents and intelligence so greatly that he had racked his brain to find a way to give her a share in the government of his kingdom. A woman as learned and talented as she could never be satisfied, Minos continued, sitting all day at a loom and gossiping.

But, Minos went on, what was he to do? While she was no doubt wise, the generals in Crete would not accept the counsel of a woman in matters of war. Nor could Minos send her on diplomatic missions—sending a woman would be considered an insult and would expose her, a beautiful young woman, to the dangerous and violent lusts of foreign men.

And so he finally realized that the best way that the queen could assist in the government was by improving the management of the royal household. Because of the unpleasantness of the stables and their steward, the palace's animal husbandry had gone neglected for far too long. The king reasoned that the queen's beauty and grace and patient heart would allow her to be indulgent of the eccentric old steward and to take control, ever so slowly and gently, of his operations. She alone could coax the steward to listen to the suggestions of others. Indeed, the elderly steward was but one bad chill from becoming a shade in Hades, and someone—the queen— must understand the management of the livestock, so disaster would not ensue upon his death. King Minos begged the queen to reconsider the importance of her new job for the long-term administration of the palace.

King Minos said that he was saddened and disappointed to hear that Queen Pasiphae was thinking of leaving the lovely palace in Knossos. Although he was a stern man, as a king must be to safeguard his people, his heart secretly melted when he saw her. He loved her dearly and would be at a loss without her. Queen Pasiphae was, of course, free to return to her father's house. But the king worried for her safety. Given her beauty and renown, another lord might seek to take her by force and violate her. Or she could be kidnapped by Crete's enemies and held for ransom. King Minos simply could not bear the thought of her being in danger.

Indeed, King Minos was certain that any lord who took her by force would claim, after the fact, that Pasiphae had been remarried of her own free will. King Minos would find himself tortured by the thought that his dear beloved was being hurt and abused. He would have no choice but to make war upon her new bridegroom and to rescue her. Such was his burden. In closing, the king hoped the queen's heart was moved by his pleas and that she would continue to help lighten His Majesty's heavy yoke of government by striving to excel in her new duties as mistress of the beasts.

Queen Pasiphae's eyes narrowed with rage. She tensed and shook slightly. She groped for words but was at a loss. Not knowing how else to respond, she forced a smile and thanked the king, her husband, for his sweet and gentle words. She reassured the king and his ministers that she had spoken in ill-advised anger and haste, and that the lack of food and drink had rendered her irritable and light headed. She begged their forgiveness and took her leave.

As she walked outside, into the hallway, Queen Pasiphae thought she heard, ever so faintly, snickering wafting away from the king's chamber. The queen devoted all of her energies to maintaining her pride. She willed herself not to hear the intermittent giggles. Nevertheless, that night she was unusually rude and demanding of the cook, and even insisted on whipping one of the servant girls for the disrespectful—no, spiteful—manner in which her food was dropped abruptly on the queen's dinner plate.

Queen Pasiphae, however, soon learned to appreciate her work in the stables. In the beginning, the king's speech had made her inspections of the stables even more bitter. She started losing patience with the steward and yelling at him that he was an incompetent old fool who wasted the time of his betters with his never ending prattle about the fine distinctions in the colors of animal urine. While these outbursts made the queen feel vengefully satisfied for a moment, the consequences were disastrous: the steward chalked the queen's ill humor up to her failure to absorb fully his wise observations and learning. Consequently, he felt it necessary to repeat all of his insights into animal management over again, even more slowly, and with extra details thrown in, as the steward had sadly concluded that his initial lectures were too subtle and recondite for her layperson's understanding.

Queen Pasiphae fell from rollicking rage to sad, mute browbeaten resignation, overcome by the steward's unstoppable barrage.

Still, Queen Pasiphae was a clever woman. When all seemed lost, she hit upon a new strategy to save herself: flattery. One inspection day she began by thanking the steward for all of his lessons and wise advice. She had learned so much from him and she was eternally grateful and would never forget his kindness in teaching her so much. She had complete confidence now in his management of the royal herds and flocks. She stroked his wrinkled, shrunken ashen cheek and smiled benevolently. But, the queen continued, she was worried that her visits were distracting the steward from his important work and depriving the animals of his nurturing hand for long periods. She felt she had learned so much from the steward already that she could now conduct the necessary inspections without interrupting him from his work. But she would still come to him, of course, with any questions or concerns.

This speech elated the old steward. After years of neglect and scorn, this was the first time anyone from the royal household had ever thanked him for his years of excellent service.

The queen slipped away, although she did not return to the palace. Instead, Queen Pasiphae walked alone—gloriously alone—to the cattle pasture where the cows and bulls fed on the great green meadow under the vast blue sky. She soon made it a regular habit to visit the cattle pasture by herself. She would stand by the fence around the meadow, her arms dreamily drooped over the edge, her body slouched, and ... and nothing. She would embrace being nothing. Only the sky and the breeze and the big, lumbering peaceful cattle.

The queen found herself growing in admiration for the cattle as she observed their way of life more frequently. She saw distinct advantages in their culture. Cows and bulls did not lecture each other, but seemed to work together in trusting harmony. Cattle enjoyed the simple pleasures of fine sun, fresh grass, and refreshing water. Cattle felt no need to make war upon any other animals, much less each other.

It was but a short step from loving cattle in general to loving a dashing bull in particular. Among the royal herd, there was one particular prize animal, a great white bull. The white bull had the most remarkable hide, a hide of bright gleaming white without a spot or blemish. Dirt and mud seemed to roll off of him. He had fantastic horns, long, sharp, and firm. He had a hulking, muscular body. While the other cattle (and many humans) instinctively feared the massive white bull and his immense horns, he was a gentle giant. He never gored or attacked anyone. His eyes seemed, to the queen, to be noble and melancholy, as if he empathized with all the world's suffering, but was saddened by his inability to alleviate so much pain.

Pasiphae gazed at him for hours in her solitary reveries. She swore to herself that the great white bull looked back at her with such tenderness in his eyes that her heart melted. She became convinced the great white bull understood her suffering heart. She wondered which god looked after the noble bulls. And how, she further wondered, can a bull appeal to the gods? It cannot make a burnt offering of its wife or neighbor on an altar—that would be, from the bull's perspective, murder. But gods are not interested in chewing grass. No, Queen Pasiphae thought, the great white bull can only appeal to the gods by displaying the nobility of his character; no bribing the gods with roasting, slaughtered meat. The great white bull confronted the gods with his simple moral truths of kindness and decency, unlike the duplicitous humans who were forced to purchase divine sanction for their wicked schemes through sacrifices of poor animals and dedications of overdone temples.

In this way, gradually, day by day, Queen Pasiphae, in her daydreams, brought herself to love the white bull. In her imagination he was her true soulmate, the other half with whom she belonged. Her marriage to King Minos, with his snickering and his jealousy, was an unkind practical joke played by the gods and not Fate's true choice. Fate intended her for the white bull. She was sure of it.

Unfortunately, the white bull did not love her in return. While casting sympathetic glances upon Queen Pasiphae's longing eyes, he only chose wives from among his own kind. The queen began to daydream about how wondrous it would be to become a cow. As a cow, she would have no cruel King Minos or tattered dignity to worry her. She could roam, lazily, across the meadow. She would have all the time she wanted to rest and reflect. She would only need to find a comfortable little patch of grass for a solitary repast, and all her bovine yearnings would be satisfied.

Queen Pasiphae knew, of course, exactly who her husband would be if she were only a cow—the great white bull. She would reject all other suitors—not rudely and contemptuously, like a spoiled human beauty, like Pasiphae herself only a few years back, but gently, tenderly, as befits a sweet, peaceful cow. She would gingerly and submissively approach the great white bull. He would look upon her with his gaping, warm eyes and embrace her offer of unconditional, eternal love.

However, something—an itch or a memory of an errand that she had passed off to a servant—would jolt Queen Pasiphae from her pastoral dream, and she would realize that she was a human woman. She would swallow her saliva hard and curse her fate.

Why, Pasiphae thought, could she not become a cow? Didn't one of the gods—Zeus or Ares or Apollo—she got confused sometimes among all the different deities—transform himself or his love or both into a bull or cow? Did the gods not constantly punish mortals by changing them into beasts—like the poor man who peeked at Artemis bathing and was hexed into the body of a deer? If the gods had the power to transform people into animals to punish them, then surely the gods could transform her into a cow so she could be the wife of her true beloved and lead the peaceful, sweet life she knew she was meant to lead.

To which god should she turn? Not the male gods—they would not understand. Male gods had cold hearts and hot lusts like mortal men. Athena would not do, either—too warlike—probably impressed with King Minos's brutal warfare. Artemis was also quickly rejected: the goddess of the hunt could not be expected to understand the need to protect and love animals like the wonderful cattle. Hera, too, was a bad idea—a jealous queen who would likely view Queen Pasiphae's transformation as some sort of ruse by her husband Zeus to lay with another mortal woman. So Queen Pasiphae settled on the goddess Aphrodite, goddess of love, who would know the pain of a longing heart. She convinced herself Aphrodite would hear her prayer and transform her and end her suffering.

Queen Pasiphae began to pray fervently at Aphrodite's temple in Knossos. She made great sacrifices in her honor, although never of cows or bulls; Aphrodite's divine nostrils were bathed in the scents of lamb meat. Pasiphae ordered the temple to be renovated and redecorated at her personal expense. The priests greeted Queen Pasiphae with eager, subservient smiles and loudly trumpeted her newfound piety.

The queen's religious fever burned for a month or so. Then, in despair, she realized that her prayers were not being heeded. The goddess of love had scorned her and her dreams. The gods' power to transform humans into beasts was fine as vindictive sport, but not to ease the queen's suffering. Pasiphae coiled her body in her bed, poured her tears into her pillow, and silently cursed the indifferent gods.

The next day she returned to the meadow. There he was, her true love, the great white bull shining beautifully in the sun. He moved heavily but gracefully. He looked at her and then hung his head down. Queen Pasiphae was certain the great white bull had been full of hope, but now he shared her despair.

Desperation is a dangerous emotion. A plan came together in Pasiphae's addled mind. The queen decided to summon a witch. She called an old servant to her, the kind of superstitious old crone Pasiphae knew could locate a reputable and discreet witch. Pasiphae told the maidservant that, with the king's imminent return from a foreign war, she wanted to try again to give him a son. Her womb, however, had remained stubbornly closed. Could she find a witch who could perhaps offer some help? The old maid said that she knew just such a woman who lived a little outside the city. If the queen would give her three days, she would find this woman and smuggle her into the palace. The queen readily agreed.

During these three days of waiting Pasiphae could barely sleep or eat. She paced the fence around the cattle's meadow restlessly, with a somewhat deranged and uneven gait, tripping every now and then. The steward was alarmed and offered to send for a doctor, but Pasiphae shooed him away brusquely.

Finally, on the third night, the witch arrived at the palace and was ushered into the queen's bedroom. The witch was an unusually small woman, her head barely reaching over Queen Pasiphae's waistline. She had little flesh left on her bones, and what was left had been kneaded into intricate folds of dry wrinkles. To support herself and keep her tiny frame from being swept away, the witch leaned on a wooden cane almost as tall as herself. As the queen's chairs were too high and cavernous for her, the witch picked a spot on the floor and planted herself there cross-legged. She looked up serenely at Queen Pasiphae, who was perched on the edge of her bed. Pasiphae, without realizing it, was tapping her foot violently.

Queen Pasiphae broke the silence and addressed the witch: Dear Mother, thank you for coming. I must take you into a terrible secret. You must swear by the gods never to reveal my secret. I will make you the wealthiest woman in Crete, but first swear to me that nothing I say will pass from your lips.

The witch swore an appropriately solemn oath by an appropriately wrathful god.

Thank you, kind Mother. I have come to you because I love another other than my husband. And I love this other so passionately. He is not a king or a lord, but a simple soul who loves to walk in the grass and admire the sun. I have no wish to harm my husband, but merely to transform myself, to become someone different, the someone I would rather be, so that I can slip away from this life and join my beloved.

The witch looked at the queen's pleading eyes. She sighed and offered her counsel: Child, I can change your appearance, but you must be careful. Men are fickle. Your beloved clearly finds you beautiful as you are now. But, if I change your face, your hair, your eyes, will he still love you? You must choose your new mask carefully. Do not trust in a man's loyalty.

The queen extended her hands and studied her nails. She paused to collect her thoughts. She began to speak, stopped herself, and then sighed. She looked even harder at her nails, which had recently been painted dark blue, as if they contained some great hidden wisdom. The witch was patient and quiet, and watched her without expression.

Having weighed her thoughts, Queen Pasiphae replied:

If only it were that simple. My beloved is not a man, he is a great white bull. I want to be a beautiful cow, the most ravishing and alluring cow that ever lived, and to be his wife. Can you do that?

The witch straightened her back and looked up at the ceiling. She paused. When she spoke again, her voice was halting: You want to be transformed into a beast? Witches, like gods, punish our enemies by making them into foul beasts. The consequences can be terrible, but of course I can do it. I can mix a potion and recite an incantation to make you a cow. You must understand things never end happily with such magic. Listen. I once knew a woman who wanted to be transformed into a man because her beloved's heart inclined only towards lovely young men. She ignored my warnings and insisted, so I changed her. As a man she was promptly drafted into the army before she could even try to seduce the man whom she loved, and she, now he, was laid low by an arrow in her—his—first battle.

Another poor soul was in terrible debt and asked me to transform him into a bird for three days, just enough time to fly away from his creditors and find a new home. In his second day as a bird, the fool, inexperienced as he was at flying, got his left wing tangled in a tree branch and was killed by a hungry urchin looking for easy prey for his lunch.

The gods will see to it that we each receive our fate and just portion. Magic can help ease your burdens, quicken your path to where you belong when used correctly, but you cannot escape yourself. No metamorphosis can change your fate. No flight into another body will undo the black ruins of your life.

The queen, however, continued to insist on being transformed into a cow.

But, Your Majesty, how can you be sure that you are right? You are passionate, angry, confused. Clearly you have some trouble with your husband, I do not want to pry but I am an experienced woman, I understand the plague that a husband can be. You do not know what it will really be like to be a cow. Perhaps you will hate it? You will miss beds, sheets, dresses, human company? Maybe you will long to see a relative someday, a parent, a sister, and then what will you do? There are no banquet couches for cows. You will be slaughtered for the evening meal if you show up. You cannot escape all the bonds tying you to the human world.

I am losing my patience, witch. Yes or no?

The witch thought to herself, she is a stubborn one. Usually they come to their senses by now. Then the witch hit on a clever idea: Your Majesty, if I may make a suggestion. I can mix a potion that will make you a cow, but only for two days. After two days the spell will wear off, and you will be human again. With this brief taste of cattle life you will be in a better position to make an informed decision about whether you want to be a cow or a woman.

Queen Pasiphae agreed. Two days later the witch returned early in the morning with a small vial containing a purple shiny liquid with a thin consistency. The queen paid her lavishly and dismissed her. She passed an impatient and distracted day in which she had to feign interest in human matters such as planning a banquet for a visiting lord from the countryside, although her mind could truly think of little but the bliss she anticipated once she shed her human skin.

When night fell at last, Pasiphae sneaked away from her tower in the palace complex and towards the cow pasture. She climbed over the meadow's fence, lay down, and looked up at the bright stars. The world seemed at peace amidst the workmanlike humming of the crickets, and she felt a love for all nature. The queen drank the vial and drifted off to sleep.

In her dream she felt her skin bulge, tighten, and roughen into a hide. Her eyes grew bigger; a tail sprouted from her back. Her hands and feet clumped together, hardened, and grew into hooves. Her mouth opened, nibbled some grass, and it tasted sweet. As the sun rose, so did Pasiphae, who now found herself transformed into a lovely large cow, although she retained her human mental faculties. She was overjoyed.

The other cattle soon joined her in the meadow. She was so happy. She walked around trying to make friends with the others. However, they either ignored her or shunted her away. The queen chalked this up to her poor understanding of bovine etiquette. With time, she figured, she would learn the correct way to charm lady friends as a cow.

She saw him strutting in the pasture in the clear morning light, the great white bull who danced through her dreams. Now was her chance. She went up to him and sauntered around him in a way that she hoped was seductive for a cow; it was not entirely clear to her what was alluring to a bull. The white bull ignored her for some time. But she was persistent. Eventually, after she circled her beloved many times, he lifted his head from the tasty grass, looked at her curiously, and decided to lay with her.

Having finally loved the handsome prince of her dreams, Pasiphae drifted off that night into a deep and blissful sleep. But in her dream she felt her great cow's body shrink and soften. Her hooves shattered into squiggly fingers and toes, hard for a cow to walk on. Then she felt a bitter taste in her mouth—the grass had somehow turned vile. That bitter taste in her mouth woke her and she spit out the grass.

It was dawn and the sun was blood red. The magical stars had faded. Queen Pasiphae stood up. She was human again and quite naked. She cried out in anguish. Her wails woke the steward, who immediately summoned the palace guards. The guards brought a blanket to wrap her in and whisked her back to the palace.

In her absence, King Minos had returned from another foreign war. He had been furious that his wife was missing. While in public he made a show of grief and moaned that no homecoming could be a triumph without his wife's sweet caresses, in private he raged, convinced that she was in the arms of a secret lover, no doubt plotting treason together. Maybe even the treacherous bastard who had dared to kiss her.

Then his wife turned up, wailing and naked, in the cattle-feeding meadow of all places. King Minos was perplexed. What was this trick? Was she going to pretend she had been ravished by a god? Or perhaps she would feign madness to win sympathy and lure him into her trap, whatever it was.

Queen Pasiphae lay in bed, shivering for quite some time. Her naked lounging on the meadow in the brisk night had led to a high fever. In her delirious state she was often heard calling out to a mysterious lover, whom she promised to rejoin soon—words that wound their way from physicians' ears to servants' mouths to the ears of King Minos, whose hatred burned. When her health returned, the queen discreetly summoned the witch again. This time the witch did not come. Queen Pasiphae, who had decided upon the life of a cow, found herself trapped in her human form against her will. She cried for hours, and eventually sank into a deep melancholy. The queen would not leave her bed and only ate a little bread, cheese, and watered-down wine. Minos saw she was lovesick and concluded the worst.

And then Pasiphae's body changed once more. This new metamorphosis began with an attack of vomiting, which finally induced her to leave her bed. No matter how much or how little she ate, each morning the sickness returned and she vomited. She began to get hungrier, and demanded the preparation of specific and odd dishes, like huge plates of nothing but aged cheese. Her belly swelled quickly and she was toppled onto her bed by the enormous size of the child within her.

Now that she had given birth to her child, her large, odd monstrous child with his calf's head, she loved her baby dearly. The queen did not care about the lying words of King Minos or Poseidon's priest. Her beloved, sadly butchered on the temple altar, had bequeathed to her a child. She swore upon the great white bull's memory to care for the baby monster and to raise her beloved's son to be as kind and dignified as his late father.

II. The Boyhood of a Monster

A PROBLEM SOON arose: No one was quite sure how to raise a child that was neither entirely human nor entirely bull. There was first the question of a name. Should the child receive a beast's name, like Spot or Speedy? Or a boy's name, like Telemachos, to honor the loyal young prince whose stepfather, King Minos, had triumphed in foreign wars? The debate was surprisingly fierce. King Minos and his courtiers advocated for an animal name. After all, they reasoned, the head contains the brain, the brain determines the nature of the soul, and thus any child with a calf's head must have a calf's brain and a calf's soul. Queen Pasiphae did not have any logic to rebut these subtle points of science, but simply insisted that, when she looked into the baby's calf eyes, she saw the soul of a little boy gazing back. She claimed that when she was sad her baby wiggled up to her to comfort her; when she smiled, the baby laughed. In the end, it was decided on a compromise: he would be known as a royal prince, but one that was a beast—the Minotaur, literally, "Bull of Minos."

This was, naturally, only the first of several debates, as each step of the child-rearing process had to be reconsidered for a royal prince who was a unique and monstrous cross of boy and calf. The next debate was whether the Minotaur should be raised among people or cows. Queen Pasiphae ordered that her baby would live with her and instructed her servants to prepare a room adjoining her bed chamber for use as a nursery. King Minos protested that cows do not live indoors and that the child's inevitably filthy habits would turn the queen's soft feminine tower into a stinking stable. But the queen would brook no dissent. The king eventually concluded that any stink would be confined to his wife's apartments and would not touch his, and so let the matter rest (although he asked his wife to wear extra perfume at official events).

The queen and her servants watched the baby Minotaur carefully. No one knew how a half human, half bull baby would develop, and whether its human features would predominate. The queen's life soon revolved around her baby. Although she had felt unaffected by the spectacle at the temple of Poseidon at the time, she was assailed by waves of anger and embarrassment afterwards. Everywhere that the queen went, she was received with either exaggerated, icy formality or barely suppressed snickers. The wits in the taverns of Knossos composed bawdy, explicit ballads of the queen's bestial romp. King Minos took no steps to restore respect for his wife and even had some of the songs performed for his private amusement. He was not entirely certain what had transpired, or why; but he was firmly convinced that his wife's conduct was loathsome in some way or other. He no longer slept with her at all, and took no steps to conceal his mistresses. The queen was treated as a necessary decoration at official functions, like a good bowl, useful and lovely, but otherwise tossed to the side.

Bouncing between cold politeness and malicious remarks, the queen turned to the one person still available that did not care about her past conduct: her little baby monster. She was devoted to her child. She believed he was a miracle sent to her by the gods. She would protect him from the cruelties of the world of King Minos, his courtiers and generals, and create a better, softer world for her monster baby in her tower.

It was, in fact, quite helpful that the queen chose to devote herself to motherhood, because the child had some unusual difficulties in reaching the typical milestones of a human child's growth. The little monster had a great deal of trouble with his body: Because his calf's head was so large compared to his human infant body, it took an unusually long time for the baby Minotaur's neck and shoulders to be able to lift and control that massive head. The poor baby monster would strain and lunge and shimmy with all the might of his newborn muscles, and then cry indignantly when he had failed yet again to be able to lift his head on his own.

Although, once he finally had control of his head, the Minotaur wasted no time learning to move his arms and legs and to roll over. Learning how to walk, however, was a more challenging task. At an early age, he figured out how to pull himself up next to the furniture to stand upright like the grownups around him. Balancing his arms on the beds and chairs and couches he was able to move back and forth on his two legs. But walking without such support was hard on him. It was difficult to keep his balance with his massive calf's head. The Minotaur could not walk until he was two years old, perhaps a little more. Queen Pasiphae clapped and cried as her little baby monster took his first real, independent steps. He smiled broadly with pride. She sent a triumphant announcement to King Minos and his ministers. The king and his Court were not sure how to react. It seemed good and fitting that any prince, even a monster one, be able to walk on his own two feet. On the other hand, went some courtiers' whispers, being able to walk on his own could be the first step towards the monster becoming a threat to the safety of Knossos and Crete. An immobile monster would be easily contained. Who knew where, someday, this monster would want to walk and what he would do when he got there ...?

Queen Pasiphae was relieved that the Minotaur appeared to have a human soul. At three months he would answer coo, coo, coo to his mother's coo, coo, coo. By one year he was pointing at everything around him and demanding an explanation or at least a name. When he was ignored, he would weep. But when a kindly grownup talked to him about what he pointed to, the Minotaur's big calf eyes glowed; if the explanation was particularly deft, he clapped rapidly and boisterously.

Most astonishing to all of his caretakers, the Minotaur learned to talk. Even Queen Pasiphae had doubted whether he would ever speak, as he was afflicted at birth with a calf's mouth instead of a boy's mouth. At ten months the Minotaur began to gurgle sounds: mamamama, dadada, bababababa, gagamama. This was an encouraging sign, but no one was yet willing to believe that a calf's head could make human speech.

And then it happened one day. Queen Pasiphae was holding the Minotaur in her lap in the nursery, flanked by two young servant girls. The servants were accustomed to the strange baby monster and even made a slight fuss over him, tickling his belly and calf ears. The day was clear and lovely, and the bright sun warmed the nursery with its light through the window, which faced the palace gardens. These gardens were a large interior courtyard dotted with trees and flowers and gently paved gravel paths. A great fig tree grew near the nursery window and a branch of the tree reached just inside. Perched on the branch that day was a small red bird. The bird walked down the branch until she was facing the nursery's inhabitants. She looked pensively at them and cocked her head quickly to one side. The humans paid her no heed. Still, the little bird judged this group—three women and one baby monster—to be a suitable audience for her art and burst into a melancholy song, a sad lament, perhaps for a fledgling lost from her nest, now settled in some other tree.

The Minotaur raised his head to look in the direction of the song. He pointed at the little red bird. He bopped up and down a bit with a broad smile on his face. The women smiled indulgently at his enthusiasm. Then it happened:

Burd, burd, burd, the baby monster cried.

The women looked down at him. They did not believe they had heard correctly; maybe they had imagined it. So Queen Pasiphae leaned over to her monster son and asked, softly, Sweetie, what is that singing so pretty? She pointed to the little bird.

Burd, burd, burd, burd!!!! He cried, waving his hands about in the air and kicking his feet. He smiled at his mother. She jumped back and put her hands over her mouth. She looked at her two servants and gestured with her index finger at the baby and then at the bird. The two servants nodded, and were so stunned they could not summon any words.

Burd, burd, the baby monster continued, clearly quite proud of himself now, and relishing the attention that he was receiving.

Soon other words followed: mama, ball, sun, shoes, fig, and other similar simple words. More and more complex words followed. Then short sentences and then longer ones. By two-and-a-half years of age the Minotaur spoke as well as, if not better than, any human child who was his age.

The Minotaur's human-leaning development raised two questions for the perplexed grownups taking care of him. First was the matter of food. He had always drunk milk from his mother's breast, supplemented by bottles of fresh cow's milk. It was the judgment of the queen's personal physician that the child should receive both variants of milk, as it was unclear what he would need from each. He should get the nurturing sustenance from both kinds of loving mothers, the physician had advised, trying to be diplomatic about his unusual patient.

Now the Minotaur was growing too big for milk. The toddler monster greedily devoured pureed vegetables, especially green vegetables. But he spit up any pureed meats. Indeed, the queen's household soon learned that the little monster was a strict vegetarian. He preferred raw vegetables to cooked ones, and was soon feasting upon the leaves from the fig tree branches that overhung the nursery window. Queen Pasiphae surmised that the Minotaur took after his father's culinary habits and she directed her servants to go each morning to the cattle herd's grazing pasture to pick fresh grass for her monster son.

The second question was how the young monster would be educated. Queen Pasiphae thought that he was a smart, curious, and charming little boy, like other little boys his age, except, in her view, somewhat more gifted. He had a strange-looking head and ate odd foods, it was true, but she pointed to his faculty of speech and his budding soul. He asked so many questions about everything he saw. This, to the queen, was definitive proof the little monster boy deserved a regular noble boy's education with other noble boys his own age.

King Minos overruled his queen this time. The boy was a monster, he would terrify the other pupils. Just look at him. And, the King continued, no one knew if or when the Minotaur's human side may subside and he would be seized with the spirit of a violent bull. He was already unusually tall and muscular for his age. Should he become agitated and bestial, the little Minotaur could easily maul several little boys. The king could not risk it. The boy would stay confined to the queen's suite of apartments.

The king did, however, agree that the boy would be educated, to a degree. He summoned an old, retired teacher, a man with a reputation for tenderness. He had a weathered face and tired grey eyes. He was to visit the Minotaur twice a week and teach him reading, writing, and basic arithmetic. At first, the tutor was nervous in the presence of a little monster; his teaching experience was, unfortunately, limited to fully human boys. He would not sit alone with the Minotaur, but insisted on the presence of a royal guard, a bored hulking giant in clanging, loud metallic armor. The bright glare of the reflected sun from the armor and the loud sounds of the restless metal movements made the little Minotaur hide under his blanket or run crying to his mother. Queen Pasiphae eventually persuaded the tutor he was in no danger from a small boy, even if the boy's head was strangely shaped and on the large side.

The tutor, nevertheless, kept his distance. He would not sit down next to the Minotaur, but always on a chair opposite his pupil. The chair was kept at a distance of a grown man's arm or more. The tutor conducted his lessons in a rapid fire monotone and made his visits brief. He mostly assigned lessons to be completed independently, checked the work on the next visit, and quickly went over the new assignment. He did not linger with the Minotaur and politely rebuffed the queen's attempts to draw him into conversations or longer visits. He was always pleading some new urgent appointment or errand, even though he had retired from active life. His breathing was somewhat labored when he was with his monster student, and the tutor rarely looked the Minotaur in his calf's eyes. When his pupil asked questions, the tutor either answered tersely if the question was a simple one: What do you get when you add ten and ten? Or he told the little monster boy to focus on his lessons and stop daydreaming when the questions seemed less comfortable: Why can't I visit the gardens below? They're so pretty.

The Minotaur complained to his mother that the tutor was mean, but he dutifully went through his lessons. After the Minotaur mastered reading, writing, and basic arithmetic, which was not long (despite his off-putting appearance, the little monster was a quick study), the queen happily discharged the tutor and decided the Minotaur would continue his studies independently, using the resources of the palace library. She wanted no more assistance from the cruel outside world. She wanted nothing to hurt her boy monster, and nothing to pollute the atmosphere of kindness she sought to cultivate in her tower.

The Minotaur grew up a lonely and dreamy little boy in the nest of his mother's apartments. His room was shaped like an oval and had a high ceiling. There was one window on the side with fig tree branches poking in and pointing; it faced the palace gardens below. The young monster used to spend hours gazing at the palace gardens. There were fig trees placed throughout, which grew tall, several times the size of a grown man. Below the fig trees were bushes with flowers exploding in color—blue, red, yellow, purple, pink—dazzling and bright in the sunshine. Between the flowers and the trees there were paved winding paths that curved through the garden enclosure. The paths never went straight, but tossed and turned the walkers in a zigzag of undulating curves. To the right and the left of the paths were green tufts of grass.

The garden was also decorated with beautiful statues, in white and green and pink marble. These statues depicted all things nautical as befitted a great power like Crete, which owed its might to the dominion over the seas: Nereids playing, Poseidon with his trident, heroes posing on the prows of great boats, sirens and mermaids. To ensure the singing of the sirens, those statues surrounded steadily flowing fountains and little bird houses, which attracted impromptu choruses of nightingales.

At three points in the large garden, forming a perfect equilateral triangle when viewed from the watch posts on the palace ramparts, were pavilions. Here strollers could rest, admire the view, nap, and perhaps have a small picnic. The pavilions were made of wood and painted a light sea blue. They had no walls, just a few slender columns, but nevertheless offered well-made floors and roofs and benches and tables. On the underside, hanging over the pavilion's guests, was beautiful artwork. One piece was a wondrous painting of dolphins splashing and playing in the water. Seashells were hung on the columns to complete the immersion into the imaginary seascape.

The Minotaur used to look out upon the garden and dream about joining the marble sailors on their marble ships, or swimming with the mermaids. Sometimes the pavilions were fortresses where the lovely sirens were going to be imprisoned and he, their mighty and noble champion, would have to save them from their wicked captors. The young monster always dreamed himself into the figure of a dashing and unbeatable hero.

The little boy monster would see men and women strolling in the gardens and longed to join them, but his mother said it was forbidden. The Minotaur would point to little boys and girls in the gardens playing hide and seek, but his mother still said no, but would not discuss why despite his continued imploring. These talks left the little monster boy feeling sad and uncertain about why he was subjected to such unfair, cruel treatment. He soon gave up on arguing with his stubborn and inexplicably mean mother.

When the Minotaur turned his calf's head away from the window to avoid being gnawed at by jealousy of all those other little boys below, he had more vistas to move his imagination. Around the walls were painted pictures of mermaids and sirens playing, laughing, arguing, and teasing sailors in passing ships. The colors leaped and danced in joyous exultation at maritime life—bright blue skies, luminous pink white skin, greenish blue waters, and, for the mermaids, fins of pink and orange and purple.

On the floor, mosaics were laid out in a pattern to resemble dolphins, splashing and jumping. To the Minotaur, they seemed quite happy and carefree, and utterly uninterested in the worried land-dwellers constantly stepping on them. The little monster boy sometimes writhed around on the floor pretending to be one of them having a great adventure. The Minotaur and his dolphin comrades would swim across the seas and find evil pirate ships. The dastardly pirates had taken one of the beautiful sirens captive and it was up to them to secure her freedom. The Minotaur would shrewdly deploy his troop of dolphins to surround and surprise the pirate ship and capsize it. The grateful siren would jump back into the water and hug and kiss the Minotaur in gratitude. And in these nautical fantasies there were no other little boys with special privileges granted by nicer mothers, which were denied to the little monster boy.

The high ceiling was painted like the stars at night, no moon or clouds, but just a sheet of stars upon which the little monster would trace the constellations. He loved especially to pick out Perseus and Andromeda. The noble hero was forever comforting the demure and grateful princess for her near death at the hands of a terrible sea monster. The Minotaur admired the courage of the hero in slaying a monster and saving the princess. In his boyish dreams, the young monster was always the brave hero, never the terrible sea monster, with whom he sympathized not one whit.

The room was spare in its furnishings. There were a bed and a small dresser in the corner, and an unadorned wooden chest, which had not been effectively sanded down and was a minefield of splinters. But most

important to the Minotaur was his desk in the opposite corner. On the desk
he always kept an unruly and almost toppling pile of scrolls. He spent hours
at this desk reading stories of heroes and monsters and witches and adventures of gods and great deeds. In the Minotaur's youthful imagination he
had a huge cast of magical friends: dolphins, mermaids, sirens, nymphs,
centaurs, heroes, princesses, and even a reformed and chastened pirate or
bandit now and then.

Sometimes these scrolls were not enough or he would grow tired of
reading the same ones again and again. The Minotaur would then summon
one of the elderly maids in his mother's service. This woman was small and
pickled and had little hair left, which she hid under a dirty white linen ker-
chief. She walked unsteadily with a cane, and her joints ached terribly. She
had no teeth left, and so she spit when she talked. She was long since past
the age when she could actually perform any productive duties in the
queen's household. Queen Pasiphae kept her around because she had no
family, no place to go, and perhaps the gods would appreciate this act of
charity.

As a little girl in her village in the countryside, she used to listen to the
women entertain each other with stories as they spent tedious hours at the
spinning wheel or stove while their men worked in the fields. These stories
had a different flavor than the ones in the scrolls. In the scrolls the language
was lovely and the text never veered from virtue, wisdom, heroism, and
piety, or their wicked opposites. No one dressed, ate (unless it was a magical apple), used a chamber pot, felt bored, got stuck waiting somewhere, or
was bothered by a toothache.

These were the bits and pieces of the old maid's stories. She too told
of heroes and princesses fighting monsters and braving the seas. But her
heroes and princesses were perpetually bumping into the silliest problems.
The hero would be ready to fight the monster when the monster would
ignominiously retreat because of a toothache and a need to find a monster
dentist to pull the tooth. Or a princess was ready to be rescued, except she
had eaten too much fruit at dinner and had the runs and could not get herself off the chamber pot. Or maybe she did get off the chamber pot, but the
hero fell out of love with her because her constant flatulence created such a
whirlwind of stink he could not stand it any longer. The princess would be

secretly abandoned to her pungent devices while the hero slipped away to find a maiden with better hygiene.

Throughout these stories, the little Minotaur would giggle and squirm delightfully and shout that is so silly, Yaya! (He called her Yaya as if she were his real grandmother.) The old maid would then pause. Her face would assume a serious, frowning, truly severe pose. Her arms stopped flailing about as they did when she told a story, but instead sat rigidly on her lap. She straightened her back. Her eyebrows arched haughtily. And then she announced: A hero is never silly. Then a smile would crack on her old creased mouth. This performance never failed to induce a round of ecstatic, uncontrollable giggles from the little monster boy.

The old servant woman took it for granted that the world was filled with marvels like the young royal prince with the monstrous head of a calf, but that those marvels and monsters still needed to eat and burp and get through tummy aches. So it seemed perfectly natural to her that a child monster would love what any other child would love. That was, after all, the point of her tales.

In his loneliness, the Minotaur did what any boy would do: he became an intrepid explorer of the palace grounds. The palace complex was massive, mighty, and imposing to grownups. It was the largest phalanx of buildings on Crete and a cluster of buildings and fortifications meant to overawe subject peoples and rival powers. To a small boy, even one with an oversized calf's head and eyes, this was an enchanted forest of stone and wood that had to be discovered.

The first explorations were around the tower where Queen Pasiphae had her suite of apartments. The Queen's Tower, as it was known, was circular and five stories high. The Minotaur and Queen Pasiphae lived on the fourth story. The queen's rooms were decorated in the same riot of color and maritime illustrations as her monster son's room. Her rooms were larger and airier, though, and filled with wondrous scents. As befits a queen of a great kingdom, Pasiphae had a cabinet full of exquisite, imported perfume bottles from Egypt and Phoenicia. The little monster boy loved to sneak in and gently undo the bottle stoppers and sniff them. He would close his eyes and try to imagine where each smell came from— this one a pretty beach at sunset, that one a tranquil night at sea after a storm, perhaps the third scent was the lingering feel of a scorching late summer afternoon.

When he had exhausted the possibilities of his own floor, the Minotaur decided to see what was in the floor above. So one day, as Queen Pasiphae napped, he slipped away to the staircase and slowly walked up. His walk was slow and tentative; he was unsure what awaited him. He gripped the banister tightly, even scraping his palm slightly. The Minotaur wondered what could be hidden on the top floor: Treasure? A witch? A monster?

Carefully, deliberately placing one foot up to the next stair level and trying to see in the dark bending corridor, the Minotaur took an unusually long time to mount the flight of stairs. Finally reaching the top, he found himself on a small, bare, grey stone landing. The door to the adjoining room was open, and a dull grey sunlight rested lightly and tenuously on the landing. The little monster heard drops of water falling somewhere, which made his muscles contract each time, his muscles reflexively keeping time with the drops.

The boy monster gathered his courage and went into the unknown room. Expecting and wanting and fearing what he was sure would be a great peril, which would test his budding hero's soul, the Minotaur experienced a sharp disappointment at just how ho-hum and colorless the world could be. There was no one on this floor at all, much less a monster or a witch. Nor was there any treasure. The floor was one big open room. The sun's glare in the narrow slit windows was met by a thick mist of brownish dust floating lazily in the air, giving the room a dulled light that could lull one to sleep. The Minotaur coughed several times from the dust; his eyes stung. In the big wide space there were chests and boxes and bags all strewn about. Inside the chests and boxes and bags was more junk—old broken jars and cups, torn and stained clothing, discarded bottles of perfumes and cosmetics, and other assorted knickknacks. There was nothing enchanted here. The floor was a graveyard of dated and worn objects that had been taken for granted during their brief, useful lives. Nothing decorated or painted—just everyday workhorses of the household variety, not lordly painted vessels. These pieces had clearly been treated roughly and regularly beaten. The little monster boy felt a pang of sadness that such loyal, dependable things, which had done their jobs without complaint, should be tossed aside, cracked, and forgotten so thoughtlessly. The child monster felt that the broken, dusty objects were accusing him of some treachery or crime, although he was not sure what it was. Perhaps, he thought, they were upset at being denied an honorable burial.

The Minotaur's oddly guilty conscience made the top floor an uncomfortable place to remain. Next he tried his luck downstairs in the tower. On the third floor there was a kitchen, pantry, and dining room for the queen's use. A functional but humdrum place—bare white walls stained with soot from the stove, plain stone floors, simple couches and tables. This floor was presided over by Queen Pasiphae's cook, a heavyset grumpy woman who did not appreciate the little monster's presence in her domain and did not want to watch him instead of her pots. She reached into the pantry, grabbed a huge bag full of grass and threw it to the Minotaur in a quick one-handed motion, barely glancing at him. The bag fell to the floor at his side. The little monster boy looked at his feet silently and then scooped it up. He felt wounded and quietly stepped back to the landing on the stairway. But he still greedily devoured the wonderful grass. The cook really did have a gift for her art: She had expertly seasoned the grass with shredded radishes and olive oil and a subtle hint of pepper.

The second floor was an even greater disappointment. As soon as the Minotaur opened the door and peaked one great calf's eye in, quietly and slowly, he was greeted by celebratory feminine shrieks and found himself being hugged and kissed and tossed about from one hand to another bosom to yet a different lap. This was where the queen's servants slept. The Minotaur tried to force a smile in the gratitude that he knew was due for this boisterous reception, but he found smiling to be hard. He wanted to run away from these embraces. The boy monster had a firm but fragile sense of his own budding maturity and was quite embarrassed at being coddled like a baby. The little monster was, in his mind, setting out on a great adventure to kill wicked enemies, and it was not the place for all these women to interrupt his somber drama with wet, sticky kisses that lingered uncomfortably on his calf's cheek.

The first floor, however, soon satisfied the child's lust for a good scare. The first floor was a reception area for the queen. It was one large open, airy room with a vaulted ceiling. The circular walls were painted with scenes of centaurs chasing nymphs and sirens tempting sailors. There were beautiful columns throughout the room, snow white and decorated with reliefs of birds and flowers. There were handsome, ornate couches in clusters of four scattered across the room, with a table in the middle of each quartet, and each had been tastefully set with a bowl of fruit and a painted vase with flowers. The tables were black covered with white geometric designs. The couches had cushions of silver, gold, and dark purple.

On one side of this great room was an exit to a hallway connecting the tower to the central palace building. The little monster boy made a run for this hallway, overjoyed to escape the tower hoping to see the whole great big wonderful castle. He ran as fast as he could until he felt himself being lifted—by two big, hairy hands, which sent him flying in the opposite direction. When the Minotaur twisted his fallen body and shifted to a sitting position, he saw three guards standing over his head with swords drawn. They said nothing, although one of them prodded the monster child with the back of his sword, checking the toughness of the hide of his calf head. Their eyes were cold and displayed no empathy for the somewhat whimpering little monster boy. The Minotaur wanted to vanish magically into the air and be away from these men with their swords and hard faces. He started to cry and scream for his mother. His eyes were soon overrun with tears. The soldiers, stunned at the monster's unexpectedly fragile disposition, fell back slightly. They had never imagined that a monster could be such a crybaby.

Soon Queen Pasiphae and a train of outraged women servants were storming up to the soldiers and browbeating them—vicious brutes, beasts, killers, monsters. Who would beat a sweet little boy who only wanted to play? If those stupid helmeted thugs would only stop and use their small brains just this once. By the gods .... The queen fell to the floor and grabbed and kissed and cradled and rocked her paralyzed small monster son, smothering his shaking, tear-stained calf's head. The monster child slowly relaxed in her arms.

The soldiers looked at the queen. They were not sure how to make the queen understand that they had acted as they were required to pursuant to King Minos's express orders. The soldiers moved their eyes from the spectacle of the angry mother cradling the upset calf's head to each other. They

awkwardly and stiffly put their swords back in their sheaths. After a short
period of silence the chief guard, or at least their spokesman, knelt down
and, at eye level with Queen Pasiphae on the floor, tried to sooth her wrath:

Your Majesty, we did not mean to harm the ... I mean your ... I mean
the young prince. But King Minos gave us strict orders that we cannot let
the Minotaur—I mean the prince—leave the tower. We have orders, you
see, Your Majesty.

Queen Pasiphae looked up. The guard's deep bass voice had been soft,
and that softness caressed her agitated nerves. I understand, she replied.
Back to your posts.

With his shakes and shivers growing less and less violent, the Minotaur
went back upstairs with his mother to his bed chamber. They sat alone together. The little monster child curled up on her lap. The Minotaur wanted
to float up on a cloud, just him and his mother, and live in a castle of their
own in the sky, where everyone would be nice and kind and there would be
no big hairy hands to throw anyone to the ground.

It was twilight, and the pink rays of the setting sun lit up Pasiphae's
delicate, poetic face. The Minotaur's great calf nose gave one last labored
sniffle. His mother whispered shoosh and ran her long, spidery fingers
across the calf's head. The little monster boy turned his head up and spoke
to her:

Why were those men so mean to me? I did nothing bad. It was not my
fault. I just don't want to be locked up here forever. It's not fair to make me
stay here.

Sweet child, there are many mean people and many unfair things. But
those men were not mean. They were just doing what your stepfather, King
Minos, told them to do.

Why is my stepfather mean to me? Why won't he let me play in the big
castle? It is so big that there has to be enough space for me to play in it
without bothering him. He wouldn't even notice me. I'm still little.

Your stepfather is only doing what he thinks is best for everyone. And
why do you want to run into the castle and leave me here all alone? So you
can be bothered by big dumb oafs in armor? There are a lot more than
three of them over there. The castle is a boring place run by grownups who
think they help everyone by being mean to lots of people like you and me.

But you don't have to be with those mean people. I have made a sweet nest here for you and me. I only let nice, kind people into our tower.

The Minotaur was sufficiently chastened to give up all thought of the castle for some time. Yet curious little boys eventually get the itch again for a new adventure. He grew restless and began to try to find a way, once more, to get into the main castle building. The little monster boy knew that the first floor was guarded. Nevertheless, he thought there must be another way. What if the tower was attacked and enemy troops swarmed in through the main entrance? There must be a secret way to escape.

For once, these boyish dreams had actually latched onto something real. The child monster decided to explore the fifth story again as he reasoned that the top floor would be the logical point of escape if an invading army breached the tower's defenses below. He rummaged around in the dusty junk and sneezed relentlessly for hours. Finally, he groped and tripped his way to the back wall. The Minotaur's small boyish human hands felt and felt until he came to a small door in one of the corners. It was locked, but the lock had rusted and with some determined heaving and hoeing and body slamming, the small monster child was able to break it off. He opened the door. There was a tunnel, pitch black and damp, but high enough to walk in. The Minotaur left the door open, snuck back to his apartment, grabbed a freshly lit candle, and then went back up and through the junk room to the newly discovered tunnel.

By the candlelight the little monster boy could see that the tunnel was about the height of a grown man and made of grey stone on all sides. The walls, floor, and ceiling were undecorated but smooth. He could only see a short way ahead, and so measured each step carefully. He walked and walked and walked for what he was certain was a great distance (although in reality it was not) until he came to an opening on the other side.

The boy monster found himself in the royal stables. The horrible smell of manure and sweat overwhelmed him. The little monster boy saw the old steward whose lectures on the coloration of animal urine once tortured Queen Pasiphae; he was soundly asleep in a corner on a pile of straw. The Minotaur felt nervous that he would be seen lurking where he did not belong. He crept back to the tunnel, covering the candle with his free hand so its light would not give him away. Once in the tunnel he walked as fast as he could without dropping the candle; the wax dripped hotly onto the back of his hand but he would not stop or slow, accepting the burns as the price of a safe escape.

Yet now that the Minotaur knew a secret route for leaving the queen's tower he could not resist putting it to use. At night he would sneak upstairs with a candle, go through the tunnel, and enter the stables. He would look at all the horses and goats and cows and bulls and wonder whether the animals would consider him one of their own, or whether, instead, they considered him a human. The boy monster decided that his human speech probably tipped him over into the human side of the divide between man and beast. Some nights the little monster boy even dared to wander to the cattle pasture where his natural parents had shared their brief love. He sampled the grass there, which he declared to himself to be exquisite, and not only for its sentimental value.

Despite his precautions and watchful—even fretful—eye, the Minotaur was discovered one night in the stables. Not, thankfully, by any more guards or other grownups, but by a young slave boy who worked in the stables and who had trouble sleeping that night. The two bumped into each other wandering through the stables, and the monster child almost dropped his candle into the straw. The human boy and the monster boy each recoiled in fright from the other. The human boy was a little younger than the monster boy and much smaller.

The human boy pleaded with the monster boy not to hurt him and not to eat any of the horses.

I don't eat horses. I eat grass. Have you ever seen a bull eat a horse? And I don't hurt people. I'm nice.

But you're the Minotaur. You eat boars and jackals and little babies. I know you do, you can't trick me.

I don't.

Liar. You do. You're a monster. You look scary and mean and you look like you want to eat me.

I'm not a monster. If I were a monster don't you think I would have eaten you by now? Do monster kids talk to human kids?

The little human boy mulled over the little monster boy's point.

Okay, you must be a nice monster then, and a person can be friends with a nice monster. But you better not turn into a mean monster. No eating me or the horses.

The little human boy sat down and took out some chicken bones from his pocket. He waved to the monster boy to sit down next to him and to put the candle on a nearby ledge. The human boy taught the Minotaur a game that involved tossing and piling up the bones. It was one of those elaborate games boys make up earnestly and care passionately about, but slip away from grownups' memories. The two new friends played with the chicken bones until dawn, when they each snuck back into the places where they were supposed to be sleeping.

The Minotaur went to bed that dawn overjoyed. He had his first real friend. Not a mermaid or nymph or dolphin dancing through his dream world, but a real little boy, just like himself, from the neck down at least.

For the next few weeks, the Minotaur would go at night to the stables to play with his friend. The monster boy made the human boy promise he would not tell anybody about him at all, never, ever, ever. The human boy swore by all the gods whom he could name (not too many, as it turned out) he would keep the secret.

But one night the Minotaur learned his one human friend had betrayed him. They were playing the chicken bone game as usual when the monster boy heard some rustling noises in the corner. What's that? Nothing. A horse farting. The thought of a farting horse made a muffled giggle escape from the Minotaur's mouth.

However, the monster boy heard the rustling again. A stifled, high-pitched laugh followed the rustling. The monster boy reached his arm over in the direction of the noise and grabbed a handful of rough dirty tunic and pulled it towards him. Inside the tunic was another little human boy who looked up at the monster child gripping him firmly; he begged not to be eaten.

The new boy and the Minotaur's human friend locked eyes. At that moment the monster boy knew he had been betrayed. Soon a small group of children, realizing there was no danger, crawled out and approached. The voices started flying in the semi-darkness of the stable in the night:

He really has a cow's head! Look at his crazy big eyes and teeth!

But how come he can talk? Cows can't talk!

Do you think he bites?

What do his ears feel like?

Or his nose? I bet it is wet and gross and full of cow snot.

I dare you to touch him.

You touch him.

Scaredy cat.

You're a scaredy cat.

Then why don't you touch his nose. I'll give you all my best chicken bones if you grab his snot and eat it, but you have to eat every last little drop, no cheating.

The Minotaur stood still, listening to the voices. He could not bring himself to speak. He wanted to run away, or to hit them all, or to scream clever insults that would strike them dumb, but he could not convince his arms or legs or mouth to cooperate. While the Minotaur was trying to un-glue himself from the floor, little hands began to crawl all over his calf's ears and mouth and nose and eyes. Voices were giggling—it's so slimy and gross, they called out. One hand poked his great big calf's eye, causing the Minotaur to stumble backward and to stop their eager, crawling fingers. Now that his legs were moving again the Minotaur ran away. In his confusion and anger the little monster boy forgot to take his candle. He ran and ran, groping and tripping in the thick interior blackness of the tunnel until he reached his bedchamber again. The monster boy pulled the blanket over his head. He felt alone. The monster boy wrapped more blankets tightly around his head and body until he felt he had descended into a new world where the air was heavy and filled with the smell of his panting breath. It was a world where the grabbing hands of little human boys could not reach.

That was the end of the Minotaur's wanderlust. He returned to scrolls and wall paintings and the bird's nest full of kind grownup women with sticky kisses that did not rub off fast enough, a little sadder and hurt, but grateful, so very grateful to all of them for those reliable sticky kisses.

III. The Monster in Love

BY THE TIME of his sixteenth birthday, the Minotaur's body had changed. On the lower, human side, hair starting creeping out of every crevice, his shoulders broadened, and his muscles widened and thickened until the monster looked like one of the king's guards from the neck down.

The calf's head grew into a true, fearsome bull's head. The monster grew horns, long, sharp, terrifying horns, which often left him grumpy and uncomfortable. Human bodies are built upon the assumption that their occupants are not carrying long sharp horns atop their heads. Unfortunately the monster's horns kept getting caught in chandeliers, bumping into doorways, and toppling over the contents of shelves. The Minotaur was continually frustrated as his bull head grew and morphed faster than he could learn to adapt it to the mismatched surroundings in the queen's tower.

The hide of the bull's head toughened and became taut. It turned coal black, losing the white spots the monster had had as a little boy. Queen Pasiphae was disappointed, as she had hoped that her son's bull-part would grow to resemble his father's shimmering white bull hide.

The Minotaur was soon far too tall for his bed and slept on the floor with his blankets. None of his clothes fit, and the tower's seamstress was exhausted from always making something new for the resident monster. As the monster kept growing out of everything, and he often ripped his delicately woven tunics with his clumsy movements, his mother decided to use only the coarsest, cheapest fabrics. These made him itch and gave him a slight rash for a time, although the seamstress successfully argued this was a small price to pay for not wasting high quality fabric upon a young prince who did not take proper care of his clothes.

With his new strength, the Minotaur helped the women of the tower carry heavy loads around the rooms and up and down the stairs. The cook was particularly appreciative as her pantry was filled with heavy bags, the weight of which had bent her back over the years. The cook's goodwill in turn was especially useful to the Minotaur as the monster's appetite was never-ending. The queen's servants were compelled to make long trips through the gardens of Knossos and the surrounding country-side to pick all of the grass and vegetables that his expanding body demanded.

The monster also felt new stirrings in his soul. He began to notice when some of the servant girls' dresses fell sideways, momentarily showing their tanned and muscular legs, before casually readjusting the fabric. The monster would feel a rush of joy, but also a knotted pain in his stomach, when long thick black scented curls brushed against him or were tossed near him, by a servant girl concentrating on some laborious task. She did not notice what mischief her hair had caused, but he certainly did.

Sometimes one of the servant girls would see the monster's great big bull eyes lingering on her and smile or sigh. The Minotaur would quickly look down or to the side and feel a desire both to stay where he was, but also to run and hide. He tried to figure out the schedules of the prettiest servant girls, so he could—always by accident—brush by them during the day. Sometimes this worked and sometimes it did not. The monster felt embarrassed about these silly immature games but he could not stop himself.

The Minotaur soon discovered that he could climb out of his window using his now powerful, grownup muscles. There was a tall fig tree with thick, sturdy branches that grew up from the palace gardens against the side of the queen's tower next to the monster's window. He would climb out the window and onto the tree branches. He started to sit on the branches at night or at sunset. He would feel the breezes and eat fresh figs right from the tree. As the monster was still up high in the tree and concealed behind dense clumps of leaves, no one in the palace gardens below took any notice of him or could even see him through the foliage.

The Minotaur yearned to walk the lovely paths and smell the flowers himself. So during the nights, when the paths were abandoned, he started to climb down the fig tree and wander through the gardens. To disguise himself, the monster wore baggy hooded cloaks and angled his head slightly downwards. These nighttime strolls became the monster's great joy. He would walk through the beautiful gardens under the moonlight, which was broken and scattered by the overhanging branches and danced playfully on the path and his cloak. He inhaled the fresh air perfumed by the flowers. The Minotaur felt wonderful walking briskly through the paths while a happy steady current of energy hummed through him. At times, the monster would take a bag of grass and leaves seasoned with olive oil and a jug of fresh mint water from the kitchen and make a picnic in one of the elegant pavilions in the garden.

The guards on the ramparts watched the monster warily, once they had figured out who the strange hooded man was that wandered the paths at night. They were poised for him to try to attack or even eat someone. But the monster stayed by himself in the gardens, rollicking and happy and carefree and harmless. The guards soon grew bored of watching the monster smile giddily at the pink and yellow flowers like a girl on her wedding day.

The monster's nighttime excursions unsettled his mother, the queen. Nothing good would come of these outings, she insisted. One of those guards will toss a spear at your hide one of these days and want to take your head home as a trophy. Stay here with me, she would say, in her softest tone; don't let your sad mother be forced to be all alone through the night.

But the monster did not listen to her advice. The Minotaur felt that his mother did not understand his need for fresh air and exercise, and that she wanted him to stay a scared little boy forever clutching the hem of her dress. However, he was a man now with a man's body and a man's spirit. The garden nights were just the beginning, he believed. He was going to do something great and heroic. He would show everyone he was not a monster, but a noble, fearsome, and yet nevertheless kind warrior. After some set of yet to be determined and planned great deeds and brushes with death, the Minotaur would return to Knossos to be cheered along the avenues by adoring crowds. He would be feted in a parade. King Minos may not like the monster, but he would respect him. Having no son of his own, the Minotaur reasoned that, once his worth was proven, King Minos would adopt the monster as his heir. He would become a wise and just king. He would give the people good laws, the best laws in the world, although his idle dreams were always rather unclear about what subjects these laws would actually address.

The monster, though, should have heeded his wise mother's warning. Those moonlit strolls in the palace gardens would leave him badly wounded in the end.

It was a night with a particularly bright and fiery, almost reddish, moon. The air was cool but not cold. The monster's head was full of happy fantasies as he wandered aimlessly about the garden paths. He was a hero, he was a king, he was a lawgiver; he was deified at his death like Heracles. He would have, if not a seat, then at least a warm welcome and a hearty slap on the back when got around to visiting the gods' palace on Mount Olympus.

While boldly vanquishing foes in these waking dreams the monster walked by one of the pavilions, and there she was. She was petite and clearly a girl of around his age. She had long, flat brown hair, which ran down half her back and a round, somewhat pudgy face out of proportion to her thin frame. Her skin was unusually pale; she must avoid the sun, the Minotaur thought. She had purple makeup smeared on in an oval around her eye sockets. The monster could smell her perfume sharply cutting into the otherwise clean, pure air. She wore a light purple dress decorated with a pattern of stars. She lay sideways on the pavilion's bench, with her knees up in the air and her legs bent. This had the effect of lifting the hem of her dress to her knees, so the monster could see the bottom half of her cleanly shaved legs. The Minotaur could not tell at what she was looking. Her head was tilted and her gaze seemed to fade into something distant, but he could not tell what it was. She made no sound except an occasional, faint sigh. The monster could not discern whether she sighed from boredom or sadness.

The Minotaur stood there in the path, staring at the girl for what seemed a long time. He could not pull his eyes away. He knew that he should move; there was danger here. What if a guard saw him and thought he was about to hurt her? Some gallant young would-be hero, someone like the Minotaur but with a human head, would no doubt charge upon the hapless, besotted monster with sword or spear. But still he could not move his feet. The girl looked so delicate in the white light. The monster decided that she sighed from sadness. Maybe she was lonely like him; perhaps they were two lonesome souls who could comfort each other. There was something gentle and sweet, but also flirtatious and inviting, about the kittenish way she curled up and bent her head and let her long, straight brown hair fall carelessly about. At one point the monster thought he saw a slight smile flash on her lips, which filled him with joy, but then it vanished and did not return.

At a certain point, the girl noticed the monster gaping at her with his hands slackly swaying and his body immobile. Panic flooded the girl's eyes. The Minotaur became scared; his heart raced. He thought quickly and whispered: Please, don't yell, don't run away, I am not going to hurt you. I like to walk these gardens at night. I am not used to company. I saw you, but I did not want to upset you. I am sorry. I can go now if you like.

Her eyes shifted from fear to puzzlement. You can talk? How can you talk when your head is—I mean, when you are—I mean—different? Yes, when you are different.

I don't know. I just can. Like you, I guess. Why are you out here to-night? The gardens are usually abandoned at this hour. Do you live at the palace?

She started to relax. The girl adjusted her body so that she was sitting upright on the bench. Her dress fell to a little more than halfway down her legs. She leaned her palms back on the bench and craned her head forward, towards the monster.

Yes, I came here a few weeks ago. I am a ward of King Minos. From his mother's side of the family.

She paused. Her tone was matter of fact. The monster was not sure what to do or to say. He desperately wanted the conversation to keep going, but he was not sure how. He had no previous experience at this sort of thing. The monster shifted his weight and felt light, tense rippling sensations up and down his arms. The girl surveyed the Minotaur with her eyes. She seemed to enjoy his attention and discomfort. She finally broke the si-lence, in a sly, teasing tone:

Everyone says you are a flesh-eating monster who can barely be controlled. They say in the countryside that King Minos has summoned the world's greatest sorcerers to cast a powerful binding spell to keep you from destroying all of Crete. And, of course, no one can harm you because Poseidon will inflict great destruction upon us all in revenge for your death. But you seem like a big scared pussycat. I think you even like me a little.

The monster blushed; blood surged to the monstrous bull's head and turned the black hide into dark crimson. He stared at his feet, somehow both excited and ashamed at the same time. The girl laughed and smiled, which made him feel relieved for reasons he could not understand. There was another pause. The monster found it surprisingly hard to breathe. To break the tension, the Minotaur asked: What is your name? How did you come to Knossos?

You are right, I am being very rude. Here I am, having heard all about you, but you have no idea who I am. Right. Proper introduction, as befits a well-bred young lady. I am the Lady Ariadne. I am the daughter of King Minos's first cousin on his mother's side. I have come to Knossos to learn the ways of the court and to find an appropriate and suitable husband. My share of my family estate is being held in trust for me and will be my dowry. If you have any suggestions for a suitable husband, please kindly submit them to the king's chamberlain for his considered and serious review.

She giggled again.

What brought you to the gardens?

Could not sleep.

Why?

I have bad dreams. I miss my father. I don't want to talk about it. Tell me, where are you imprisoned? How did you break out to haunt the gardens at night?

I am not imprisoned. I am a member of Queen Pasiphae's household. I am a royal prince of Crete. I live in the queen's tower, where I have lived all my life. I come down here through my window. See, look, over there, do you see that fig tree? Its branches go up to that window in the queen's tower. That is my bed chamber. I climb out the window, down the tree, and come here. It is lovely and peaceful here at night, and I crave the fresh air and the flowers. My room can get stuffy.

The monster looked at his feet again. He worked hard to stop blushing again, but was not sure that he succeeded. Then he made a bold stroke:

And maybe I too am in the market for a suitable bride. So long as her dowry is sufficient.

They both locked eyes and laughed.

Ariadne stood up. She was quite short. Her head came up only to the middle of the monster's chest. She put her hand gently on his arm. The Minotaur's body convulsed with pleasure, but he tried hard to hide it. He forced his facial muscles into an impassive expression.

It is time for me to say goodnight, O mighty young prince of Crete. Perhaps we will meet another night in the gardens. But I really need some sleep. I have to be pretty and presentable at some reception for some proud somebody or other visiting from Mycenae, from the Greek mainland, to-morrow. Good night.

Ariadne let her arm drop listlessly. She walked slowly off to one of the corners in the garden and was swallowed by the darkness. The monster watched her walk away. Her walk was dainty and feminine. Her sandals had a slight heel, which made her hips sway as she went.

That night the Minotaur had difficulty getting to sleep. He felt waves of hot intense arousal shoot all through his body. When sleep at last caught him in its net and dragged him down, the monster dreamed of that sweet, teasing, feminine walk and those swaying hips.

The next day the monster could not concentrate on any of his tasks. He was restless and could not tame his shaking and swaying body parts. He had no appetite, which startled the cook, who was convinced she must have lost her touch with a grass and leaf salad. The Minotaur tried to read his scrolls of adventure tales and legends, but all of his thoughts kept drifting back to Ariadne and her swaying hips drifting into the darkness. Every goddess and princess and siren and witch in the stories he read looked just like Ariadne in his mind's eye. Ariadne on Mount Olympus, haughty and proud and wearing a golden silk dress, as mortal men prostrated themselves in worship to her; Ariadne naked on a deserted beach singing beautiful lull-abies to lure sailors to their doom; Ariadne as the princess about to be fed to a hideous monster until the heroic Minotaur, at the last moment, burst in and saved her.

All of the monster's thoughts turned to the approaching night. He kept looking at the bright Mediterranean sun in anger: Why can't you get down already? Why do you keep loitering in the sky? Are you so proud and arrogant that you think everyone has to look at you all the time, you overbearing scorching bastard? Why not give the moon a chance? Hurry up, please, please, hurry up, and go away.

Night came at long last. The Minotaur climbed down into the garden as soon as he felt safe under the cover of night. The monster paced back and forth and around and over the paths near the pavilion where he had met Ariadne the night before. He was trying to think of things to talk about with her, which was proving hard. He was not exactly sure what a young lady of the palace did all day, or what one is supposed to say to her. Was it polite and charming to tell her how lovely she looked walking in the moonlight? Or would she take offense and storm off? Maybe she would take offense from some men but not others? But how could the monster know to which group of men he had been assigned?

The monster sweated, which made him anxious that he would smell foul to Ariadne. Calm, calm down, you do not want to look like a madman or stink from your sweat when she comes, he thought to himself. Occupy yourself, the Minotaur scolded his fevered brain, occupy yourself. Do exercises on the branches. The monster found a particularly strong branch from an old fig tree, jumped and grabbed it, and did a series of chin-ups to relieve the tension in his body.

However, even though he was right near the pavilion where they had met only the previous evening, Ariadne did not come. The Minotaur became worried. What if he had mixed up the pavilions? Perhaps they met at a different one, and she is waiting there and getting upset with him for not showing. He jumped down to the ground and raced to the other pavilions. No Ariadne. The monster circled the pavilions in a mad dash, like a hysterically crazed mouse running all over a kitchen floor. But still she did not show. At last, exhausted, defeated, and filled with sadness, the Minotaur climbed back up to his bedchamber and went to sleep.

The next day the monster did not feel like getting out of bed for the longest time. Everything seemed dull and stupid and boring and pointless to him in the too bright, painful morning sunlight. He did not want to talk to anyone. Queen Pasiphae asked what was wrong. Nothing, the Minotaur said. He went to the fifth floor of the queen's tower and threw the old junk around from one pile to another. He smashed some of it with his fists and feet. This made the monster feel better, although he could not say why.

The next few nights followed the same pattern: As the day waned the monster let himself believe in the possibility he would see Ariadne again that night. He grew excited. He tried to develop a list of things the two of them could talk about, or special little nooks in the garden they could explore. By dusk the Minotaur could not wait for that teasing, lingering pink disk to stop hogging the sky and to just get down to its bed for the night.

The monster would scamper down the tree outside his window and walk briskly, without a stop, through the garden, until he reached the pavilion where he had met Ariadne on that one magical night. His plans for the evening would grow more elaborate. The monster might decide to pick her a garland of flowers to put in her hair. It was not easy for him to make out the colors of the flowers in the dim light of the moon. What if he picked something that she did not like? Or that did not flatter her long, soft brown hair? He had never picked flowers for a pretty girl before, and he was worried he did not know the right way to do it. The monster agonized over each bush, studying the flowers like an expert gardener, although he had, in truth, no idea which flower was which, and why women might like some more than others.

After painstaking deliberation, the Minotaur would settle on a group of what he had convinced himself were six exquisite and perfect flowers that Ariadne would enjoy and that would flatter her skin tones, as best he could recall them. Then he would position himself in a stiff and straight pose in front of the pavilion where he was sure they had met. He held the little bouquet tightly and sweat trickled from his palms to the stems. He stood still, looking rapidly in each direction and then staring down. And then he started his cycle yet another time.

But Ariadne would not show herself again.

And once more, the monster would imagine he was at the wrong pavilion. Yet she was not in any of the other pavilions either.

The monster would go back to his bed, feeling drained of all feeling. The world felt empty of joy. Still, he kept the flowers. The Minotaur took a vase from his mother's bed chamber and filled it with water and put the flowers in. He placed the vase on his window sill. Somehow looking at the flowers reminded him of Ariadne and lifted his fallen spirits a little. There was hope eternal in flowers, the monster mused. Even though they were doomed to die in a few days.

Several weeks went by in this manner. Queen Pasiphae grew increasingly alarmed. Her monster son was curt with her, and he did not want to eat. He was clearly preoccupied with something, but would not tell his worried mother. She tried all sorts of ruses to cheer her monster son up. She had the cook prepare his favorite dishes. She brought in Yaya to tell outrageously grotesque stories of burping princesses and farting monsters. She had half of the royal library delivered to the little tower. But none of it helped. Whenever she tried to coax from him the reasons for his despair, the monster dismissed his mother with I'm fine, it's nothing, I just need some time to be by myself.

And then it happened again. The Minotaur was strolling in the gardens once more, at night; he could not stop himself from haunting his former fortuitous meeting place with Ariadne. He had only picked one flower, some long-stemmed thing he thought was pink, but he could not really be sure in the light of the half-moon. He was walking down the path, kicking some small round stone to pass the time, when he heard her voice:

Did you pick that for me?

There was Ariadne. She was coming up the other end of the path. She smiled. She took the flower from the monster's limp grip and strung it through her hair, just behind her ear. She wore a loose, simple white dress. The fabric lapped back and forth against her body in the wind, outlining now her leg, now her breast, and now her arm. The monster's eyes followed the wind's direction to look at now this part of Ariadne, and now this other.

I haven't seen you in the gardens for a while. I missed you. It can get lonely here.

I had to go on a trip. King Minos tried to betroth me to a prince from Mycenae. He was a big guy. He looked like a huge ugly boar. He had this horrible beard that was really patchy, like he had ripped pieces out of it here and there to munch on. He was drinking wine constantly and not watered down one bit. And all he talked about was hunting. He had killed this animal and he had killed that animal and how about this dead stuffed hide or that dead stuffed hide. He was so boring. And he smelled. There have to be baths somewhere in Mycenae. There are absolutely baths in Knossos and Prince Stink-bomb had no excuse for not using them before sitting down to dinner with me. I tried to smell my own perfume to keep from passing out from his stink.

Still, being a girl and a dutiful relation of His Majesty, when it comes to a husband, I get what I am given. King Minos delegated the negotiation of my betrothal terms to his court chamberlain, who felt no need to consult me in the matter. The haggling went on for days. I would get summoned to audiences with the two of them where I was inspected like cattle. Sometimes I was told to be elegant. Or sultry. Sometimes my body parts were examined—teeth, fingernails, hips. Right in front of me the two of them tapped on my teeth with their grimy, sweaty fingers and debated their quality—my gallant suitor from the mainland tried to get a bigger dowry by claiming that my teeth were yellowish and about to fall out. I tried to keep my spirits up, but each day I dreaded more and more the thought of marrying this disgusting, grasping drunken ogre.

Oh, and I had to perform for them. Let's see you spin. The wine-soaked pig said 'She'll be an ugly hag after a couple of babies. I need to know she can work for her bread.' Can you believe that? My mother stayed quite lovely after having children. I will too. But still I spun. I made him a pillow case, I think. For fun I put a pattern on it of a boar eating a fat drunken hunter's head. He did not even notice, but threw it at a servant.

Then they began debating the value of my dowry. The Mycenaean oaf thought that the land was not as fertile as King Minos claimed. And it must be run-down by now, he sneered. No lord to watch over it, the oaf opined, and the servants will be stealing everything. This is a lie. Our estates are overseen by a very honest and hard-working freedman who was loyal to my father and his family—and always so kind and sweet to me. He used to make me dolls when I was a little girl—they were mermaids I pretended were swimming in an enchanted sea in the middle of my bed. I bit my lips at the horrible lies said about him.

So the three of us and a pack of guards and slaves and retainers journeyed out of Knossos to my parents' estate. There, as I knew it would be, everything was in order. The Mycenaean drunk was impressed. I started to get really worried I might actually have to marry him. So I thought of a trick to get rid of him. I had my most trusted maidservant approach one of the Mycenaean pig's servants. At my instruction, my maid confided—or really just pretended to confide—I had been having a secret affair with a slave boy in the stables and that, as of late, in the bath, she saw hideous, swelling sores and grotesque hairy warts all over my unmentionable feminine places.

The betrothal negotiations ended immediately. Problem solved.

Of course, that stuff about the slave boy was all made up. I am a virgin. I am not that kind of girl.

I came back today. I was hoping to see you again tonight. I cannot believe that the palace's resident monster is the nicest person I have met in this city, but I guess the gods have a sense of humor just like us.

It made me sad to go home. I miss my father so much. His things were everywhere. His old rooms, his furniture, his desk and stylus, some of his old clothes were scattered about. It seemed like any minute he was going to come back home, tell me it was all a great big joke, and I would run to him and hug him. Still, I would be cross with him for playing such a cruel joke on his daughter pretending to be dead.

But he is really dead and he can't help me anymore. I am stuck here, with a bunch of mean, greedy men who want to pimp me and sell me to the highest drunken, smelly bidder. I feel like a horse at the market. Check her hooves. Tap those teeth. How long can you ride her? Will she be worth her price? I hate it. I hate being a girl sometimes.

Ariadne's eyes had started to water although no tears fell. She kicked the dirt on the ground. Then she inhaled deeply, let out a sigh, and grabbed the monster's hand. She led him to a pavilion. They sat down next to each other on the bench.

What was he like, your father? I never knew my father.

He was the kindest, gentlest, best man. He was the lord of a large estate in the countryside. As I told you before, he was a relation of King Minos. He was wise and learned and strong. He could have been one of the king's ministers or generals, but he had no interest in politics or war. He hated Knossos. He just wanted to live in our villa and oversee the farm. He thought King Minos's wars were wrong for Crete. Just because our navy is strong for now, he would say, why do we have to hurt and kill so many people? Isn't there enough suffering inflicted on poor mortals from disease and bandits and heartache without having to add marauding soldiers? We have enough here on Crete, and we should be satisfied. That is what he used to say.

He loved to walk through our vineyards. We made excellent wine. And we had great big vegetable patches. We kept a proud group of goats who gave us milk and cheese.

I am the youngest of three sisters. My older sisters were away and married by the time I could walk and talk—I was the unexpected child of my parents' old age. I had my daddy all to myself. I used to go everywhere with him. At first he would carry me or pull me along in a cart, which he called my queenly chariot. When I was bigger I would walk with him. He taught me how to read and write. My mother insisted that the usual sort of governesses be brought in to drill me in spinning and mending and cooking and all the rest of the womanly wifely claptrap nonsense. I groaned through it all, although I suppose, looking back, I learned quite a bit. The smelly pig-man from Mycenae was impressed—goes to show you what all that is good for. But I would just count down the hours until my daddy came home from his work around the estate.

Nights with Daddy were the best. We would pass around wine, or fresh goat milk mixed with honey we would heat in the fire. Our cook made amazing little nut pastries. Daddy would tell me stories for hours. I would curl up on his lap and he would tell me about his boyhood, his youth as a soldier, his father, his mother. But best of all were the legends he heard from the tenants on our lands. Wild tall tales of satyrs abducting girls and cruel nymphs imprisoning beautiful boys in trees when their love was spurned. Or great flying horses swooping all over the horizon. Or gorgons with hissing coiling snakes for hair that turned men to stone statues with the glare of their hideous eyes.

I was a rude audience. I kept interrupting my daddy. I kept telling him that the people in the stories should behave differently, in my opinion. Or I did not understand why something else did not happen instead. I don't think he ever got through a story without me interrupting him a thousand times. But he was kind and patient and understanding. At night he always tucked me into my bed, kissed my forehead, and called me his best beautiful little wood nymph.

I used to get terribly jealous of my mother. Sometimes, like all grownup couples, they wanted to be alone without me to talk or to do the things that grownups do. I hated this so much. She was taking him away from me, and it made me angry. It was not fair. Mommy and my big sisters had him all those years before I was born, and now it was my turn, and she wouldn't let me have him.

My anger at my mother grew worse when my parents fought. I don't think any couple can live together without fighting, but when I was little I did not realize that truth yet. I heard them shout back and forth, and I always took daddy's side. Mommy did not listen to him, I felt, or understand him. Why did she torture him so? Can't she see how hard he worked for all of us, so we would have a good home? I thought she was selfish and mean. I knew I would have made a better companion for him than her, with her petty recriminations and endless moody demands. But he was such a kind and goodly man. He gave in to her and he never gave mommy the scolding she deserved.

One day daddy came home from the fields running a high fever. He sweated all over, his clothes were soaked; I could see the sweat falling from his forehead. It was awful. He felt so hot when I touched him. We sent for a doctor and gave daddy cool milk to drink. He lay on the beat up old couch fading in and out of consciousness. I stood by him. I held his hand. I used a wet compress to wipe his forehead. I tried to get him to eat some grapes I had picked. I told him it would be alright, I would take care of him. My mother was too upset and confused to pay any attention to me or him. Then the doctor arrived and I was told to leave. I would not budge. Leave, my mother said, the doctor must tend to your father and you are in the way. This is no place for children. I would not budge. It took four slaves to grab me and put me back in my room, which they bolted shut. I screamed and cried for my father all night. Somehow I screamed myself into exhaustion and fell asleep.

The next morning I was gently woken by my mother. Her eyes were red and swollen, but she was composed. I have terrible news, child. Your father died. The doctor did everything possible, but the sickness had progressed too far. I don't think there was any pain—he died in his sleep. I gave him coins for the ferryman, and I am sure that his shade has crossed the River Styx into Hades by now. I know you loved him very much, but we must be strong now. Your father was an important man. There will be a great funeral. You must march with me and keep your dignity. The farmers and the slaves and the townspeople must not see us flinch or cry. We mourn with dignity. There is no point in any more tears. Tears will not snatch his soul home from the underworld.

I swallowed those words hard. She seemed so cold and unfeeling. And I knew it was all her fault. When she pulled me away from daddy he was still alive. I was caring for him. I was helping. I understood him. I just knew that she had killed him to take him away from me; she was jealous of me and would not let me have him. I burned with hate for my mother.

The funeral was a disaster. When I saw my father's body being carried I could not help myself, I ran to it, cried for him, I tried to hug his corpse. My mother grabbed me, smacked me with disgust, and sent me home. I locked myself in my room for hours and cried. I hated her so much.

The months drifted by. Our lives returned to some kind of routine. We did not speak of daddy, or of the funeral. We talked about everything that did not matter—food, harvests, clothes, errands. She never once apologized for shaming me in public. I was at a loss. I would wander around the fields aimlessly. I would sit by a pond and throw rocks in the water to watch the ripples. Just as long as I was away from her.

But one day my mother went too far. I told you about those wonderful little mermaid dolls, the ones that our freedman made for me? She took them from my bed chamber and gave them away to poor little girls in one of our villages. They had been gifts specially made only for me. She did not ask me; she did not care how I felt. I came home one day and they were gone. When I confronted her she shook me and told me that a girl my age, with her womanly breasts already grown, had no business being sentimental about silly little dolls. These tokens of goodwill go far with our tenants. I needed to grow up. At the end of this little lecture she looked so smug. She half smiled to herself in this superior way.

I smacked her hard, again and again, until I drew blood. I may not look like much, but apparently you should not get me angry. I can pack a real mean punch. I know that I shouldn't have done it, but I could not help myself. It was not my fault. I'm not the kind of person to hurt others, but there is only so much that any one person should have to take.

My mother responded by packing me off here, to Knossos, to be rid of me. She hopes that some man will grab me up, like a fine horse for sale, and she will never be under the same roof with me again. I hate her. Is that bad? Do you think I am a bad person for hating my mother so much?

Ariadne's eyes pleaded with the monster for approval. For the first time he noticed their color—a striking pale blue, clear and watery. The Minotaur was moved by her tale. She was a good daughter, he reassured her. She was not responsible for her mother's terrible behavior. No girl deserved such a bad mother.

Thank you. I am not sure I fully believe you, but thank you. You are sweet.

Ariadne started to calm down. She straightened herself and took in a deep breath. She let her hands fall to her lap.

I wish I could talk to him again. About mother. About husbands. About everything. I wish it so much.

Him who?

My father.

An idea then came to the Minotaur, a way both to help Ariadne and to ensure she would keep returning to see him in the gardens at night:

Maybe there is a way. I have read a great many scrolls from the palace library. Some of them talk about magic that can be used to summon a shade to speak to you from the underworld.

That's crazy. Magic like that is not real.

You are talking to a man who is half-bull. Magic is real. I am proof of it. We can use it. I can help you, I will figure this out. We will summon your father's shade and he will help you.

Are you serious? Do you think that it could really work? I guess if you are real then maybe other magical things are real too.

Of course it will work. Give me three days to figure it all out and get the right ingredients. Meet me back here in the gardens in three nights.

I will. Thank you!

Ariadne kissed the monster's cheek. That kiss sent his soul whirling and dancing for joy; the world seemed to spin swiftly but weightlessly. The monster watched her walk away again. The same lovely girlish walk, as he remembered it, her hips swaying ever so much with her hands daintily poised at her sides. The Minotaur went to bed that night full of enthusiasm for his new project. He would be the hero to save the beautiful Ariadne, or at least to help ease her suffering.

The monster rose the next day invigorated and refreshed. After devouring a large breakfast, he meticulously reviewed several aged scrolls in his room. The monster jotted some notes down. He made a list of additional scrolls he would need to consult and sent for them from the palace library.

The Minotaur read furiously over the next three days. He stayed pinned to the desk in his room, and instructed that his food be brought to him so that he would not have to waste time sitting down with his mother for more formal meals. He would not speak to anyone about anything other than his demands for texts or food. The monster rebuffed his mother's gentle inquiries at his door with harsh chords of no, nothing, fine, which closed off any further discussion.

The monster slept poorly during those days. He was determined to impress Ariadne and to keep her interested in talking to him, but at the same time terrified he would fail. He reflected it was probably quite different reading about magic than actually making magic happen in a dark garden corner. He would wake at night in a panic—had he missed a key text? Were his notes incomplete in some way? Up the monster would jump from his blankets. He would light a candle and in a blurry half-sleep try to decipher the obscure scrolls yet one more time.

He was haunted by what he imagined would be Ariadne's disappointed face. He saw himself, all apologies and choked slow syllables, telling Ariadne that he simply could not figure out how to summon her father's shade. She would offer kind, reassuring words: That is okay, I knew it was going to be hard to do this, I know you tried your best. But her body would shrink and slacken, and, having no more reason to speak to the palace's resident monster, she would trudge away with a heavy walk—no swaying hips and daintily outstretched palms—and that would be the end of their talks in the gardens at night.

No, no, no, the Minotaur told himself, I will not let that happen. He would force his mind to suppress the vision of that imagined heavy, sad permanent walk away. He redoubled his efforts. He put all his energy and concentration into this frantic crash course of independent study in sorcery. Every distracting sound—his mother arguing with a servant about oils for her hair, or a shout from the gardens below from little children—would send rolling waves of impatient rage through the monster's limbs. He cursed every distraction.

After two-and-a-half days, the monster believed he had figured out what was needed for the spell, which he was able to procure discreetly from the cook in exchange for moving several heavy bags of flour. Truth be told, the cook was quite relieved to see the young monster prince seeking out the company of people again.

The appointed night arrived. The monster slipped into the gardens with a bag filled with scratched out magic spells and ingredients segregated into securely sealed jars. The climb down the great fig tree that night was the final test for the monster's frayed nerves: He was terrified at every step that a jar might fall, smash, and spill, and he would be unable to work the spell as promised. Even though the monster planned for this contingency through the use of several overlapping bags to cushion any fall and to safe-guard against any jar slipping out, he still did not trust himself. He breathed hard during each tense, agonized movement.

The Minotaur breathed freely again once he had safely reached the ground with his cargo intact. He was sure he would make Ariadne so happy that night. Those pale blue eyes would look upon the monstrous bull's head with tenderness and maybe even start to look at him with something that went beyond ordinary tenderness.

This time the Minotaur did not have to wait long. Scarcely had he re-covered his bearings when he felt a slight tap on his shoulder. He turned his head and there she was, as close to him as she could be without their bodies touching, smelling of perfumes and oils and decked out in a surprisingly simple housedress, made from cheap rough fabric.

Please excuse my dress—it is from home, from the country. I thought it would make daddy's shade feel more at home. I don't want to scare him.

The two walked to a secluded corner of the gardens, under a spreading tree. The monster could not see Ariadne well, but he felt her breath lapping against his skin. The monster veered between desire and terror.

Did you figure out a way to summon my father's shade?

Yes, he assured her, and he displayed the scrawled incantations and all the necessary ingredients. Ariadne hesitated. Are we sure this is a good idea? Isn't magic dangerous? Maybe we should leave the shades in peace down in the underworld.

The magic is safe. I found these spells in several old priestly scrolls. These are shades. They can't hurt us.

Ariadne relented. Let's do the spell. If you are sure. I am trusting you.

The Minotaur felt a surge of pride when she said she trusted him. The monster emptied his bag. First, he took out a small lamp and lit the wick with some oil. It gave off a faint light good enough for completing the spell. He thought Ariadne's face, now lit up in the dark night, and focused on him, seemed like a star fallen from the sky. Second, he took out a piece of papyrus on which he had copied the spell. Finally, he removed two jars. In one jar was wine and in the other was the blood of a freshly slaughtered lamb. Ariadne wrinkled her brow at this supernatural, nocturnal picnic spread, but said nothing.

The monster spilled the wine on the ground and recited the spell in a rushed whisper. Then he spilled a few drops of the lamb's blood on the ground.

Now what happens? Ariadne's voice was tense and halting.

The spell draws the shades from the underworld. The shades will want to drink the blood and the wine. Once they put the liquids to their lips, the shades will be able to see us, and then be able to speak to us.

But how will we be able to summon just my father's shade? What if somebody else comes?

This was, in fact, an excellent question, and one that the Minotaur, in his frenzied hunt for the right spell, had not considered. The pair of necromancers was indeed soon surrounded by shades that jostled and kicked one another to drink the magic libation. Time in the underworld was apparently not conducive to developing good manners. But none of these shades were Ariadne's father. Instead, there was all the flotsam and jetsam of the Greek world. First was a fat washerwoman who treated them to a tedious harangue about how her husband was a good for nothing, how she had been a beauty in her youth and could have had any number of fine artisans—master cobblers and master carpenters, good tradesmen—but instead she went for the handsome one, who had not bothered staying handsome long after the wedding night. Instead, he had turned into a fat, lazy drunk whom she had to support. He had been the death of her and now his shade would give her no peace in the underworld, demanding that she get him this or that in Hades. Well, they were dead now, and she was not going to put up with him any longer. She had her eye on a handsome shade, who had just crossed the River Styx. He was a broad-shouldered, bearded man from Corinth whose wife was still stuck among the living and could not stop other women from pursuing her lonely husband.

When she finally had said her piece, her husband's shade approached the libation and tasted it greedily. He recounted his story: It was not his fault their life had been hard. He was a mason, a good one, but King Minos had no respect for Cretan workmanship. No, it was all about the Egyptians, look at the great things they could do with big black stones in their big sandy desert. So he and all the other Cretan masons were thrown out of work. Did his wife, his helpmeet, show any support, a kind word? No! That harpy would sink her claws in and nag and criticize. Was it any wonder he had turned to the one friend who had never let him down, a good jug of wine?

The Minotaur and Ariadne eventually were able to shoo him away, but it was no use. The crowds of shades kept coming. There was the baker's wife who kissed his apprentice behind her husband's back; the tutor who gave wisdom to his beautiful young charges only to be spurned for younger men; parents who came to complain about their ungrateful children who neglected them in their old age and to whom they demanded stern messages be sent by the two harried, fatigued living souls to whom these complaints were now addressed.

The blood and wine mixture ran out at last and the shades slinked away back to their homes in the underworld. The monster looked at Ariadne. She had fallen to the ground and sat cross-legged. Her shoulders drooped down. She was making meaningless shapes in the dirt with her finger. The Minotaur tried to console her:

I'm sorry Ariadne. I wanted to bring him back to you. I tried, I'm so sorry. Please don't give up. The magic works, but we are learning how to use it. Maybe it will take a couple of tries to get the spell to work right.

Ariadne looked up and sighed. You are such a sweet thing. We should try again. Let's not give up. She forced herself to smile and stood up. In two nights the monster replied. She took the monster's hands in hers. She squeezed them, smiled again, and wished him good night. Once more the monster watched her walk away, with her hips slowly swaying in the dim moonlight and her back poised in a straight arc.

The next day he was back to work. The Minotaur demanded ever more obscure scrolls. For the first time, he exhausted the deep shelves of the royal library. Messengers were sent to the temples in Knossos to find and borrow the necessary volumes in the name of the royal household.

The monster sat at his desk in his room for hours, slept little, and only communicated with servants to order food, scrolls, or candles. His eyes burned and his head throbbed, but he could not stop; he was terrified of Ariadne slipping away because he had failed in his task. His mother would stand at the doorway and look at his tense, rocking body from a distance, and see the sweat stains blotting the upper back of the cloak he had not changed for days. Still, she was not able to summon the courage to interfere. Her son ignored her.

The time of the next night meeting with Ariadne in the gardens arrived. The Minotaur was certain that he had solved the problem. Ariadne looked at him hopefully; she flashed a smile of encouragement. He spilled the wine and recited the first spell. But this time, after spilling the wine, he recited a second spell and threw three locks of Ariadne's hair into the little puddle. Only one shade started to surface instead of a crowd. Ariadne's face glowed with excitement as the shade bent down to drink.

Yet it was not her father. Instead, they had summoned the shade of a long dead cousin of Ariadne. This cousin wanted to have a word with her.

He insisted angrily that Ariadne's grandfather had cheated him. The unhappy shade launched into a long disquisition on the intricacies of Ariadne's great-grandfather's will and how it had been distorted. In particular, apparently a late executed codicil was read as being in conflict with and superseding an earlier clause that would have given this fellow title to what were now the vineyards and wine presses on Ariadne's family estate. The man retold each of the twists and turns of the probate case in the law courts, first in the province, then in Knossos before the king's counselors. He had seemingly forgotten no detail, and he would not desist until his tale reached its conclusion with Ariadne's grandfather allegedly stealing this man's inheritance. In the end, he demanded that Ariadne make amends to his heirs. Ariadne then calmly pointed out, with a touch of wicked and mischievous glee, that he had no heirs: His only son had died childless. The shade stormed off in disgust, saying he was going to have to find where his son had scampered off to in the underworld and have a word with the boy.

We are getting closer. We know that we can summon people who are only your relatives.

Ariadne sighed and laughed briefly to herself. Let's try again tomorrow night. Once more she squeezed his hands and walked her alluring slow walk away.

The next night the monster returned more determined than ever. He had found even more scrolls. He had added a new step involving a goat's bladder. But, surprisingly, that night when Ariadne came she was smiling broadly, and her features were relaxed.

You can put away all those ingredients and spells.

Why?

Because I spoke to him. To my father. Everything is well now.

How? Did you try the spell by yourself?

I had a dream vision. Last night. I went to sleep and my father's shade came to me in my dream. He caressed my cheek and called me his beautiful little nymph again, like he did when I was a little girl. He told me that the great god Hades had directed him to speak with me because my spells—that is, your spells—were interfering with the good order and efficient administration of the realm of the dead. Too many shades trying to get topside, he explained, wreak all sorts of havoc in the underworld. The smooth functioning of the underworld requires a firm demarcation between the living and the dead. He would speak to me as long as I promised to stop bothering those who should be at rest. Of course, I agreed at once. I told him I had never wanted to stir so many shades. I only longed to speak to him because I missed him so terribly.

My father asked me what was troubling me. I poured my heart out about everything—my mother's cruelty, my terror at being sold like livestock to some hideous man in a foreign country. He smiled at me and stroked my hair. We all must submit to our fate as best we can, he told me. Be brave, don't flinch, and live the best life that Fate lets you live. He promised to come to me in my dreams whenever I need him—just as long as I never use those summoning spells again.

So thank you, thank you so much. Your spell did the trick in the end. I spoke to my father. I have him back in my dreams whenever I need him. I don't know how I can ever repay your kindness. You are so sweet to me when nobody else even seems to care a thing about me. You are a real friend. Thank you.

Once more the blood rushed to the face of the monstrous bull's head, and the black hide was stained with crimson. His eyes turned to the ground. His big toe made circles in the dirt through his flimsy, worn sandals. The monster addressed his words quietly to the circles in the ground:

I want to be able to keep talking to you, to see you on more nights in the gardens. Will you come back to see me in the gardens at night? It can be lonely for me at times.

Ariadne agreed to meet the monster two nights each week, in the gardens. She could not meet too often. She needed to be circumspect. She had to maintain her reputation as an upstanding virgin, or the quality of prospective grooms would slide even further. Too many nighttime constitutionals would eventually raise too many eyebrows. Anyway, she was busy on many nights at official palace events where she exhausted herself in the effort to be charming and enticing, but still chaste and submissive, to all those men swirling about the room—and none of them seemed to appreciate how hard their conflicting desires were to appease. She knew that the Minotaur would understand.

He nodded with a blank stare on his face.

The monster pined impatiently for those precious few garden nights with Ariadne. The days in between felt lifeless to him. The only real life, the monster thought, were those garden nights with Ariadne. She would speak for hours and hours. Once Ariadne started to speak, she could not stop. Court decorum forced her to be quiet and demure when with company, especially overbearing, arrogant, boastful male company. Even amongst the other women her own age she had to watch her tongue—enemies were everywhere and a noble young lady would gladly trade some juicy malicious gossip for a better chance at grabbing the husband whom she wanted. But Ariadne could speak freely to the Minotaur. Nobody gossiped with monsters. And he was such a wonderful listener.

Ariadne complained at length about the other women at King Minos's court. This one deceived her husband and slept around with other men. No one would tell her husband, but everyone made cruel jokes about his foolish devotion to her. That lady with the now-wrinkling skin around her lips and eyes was jealous of the beauty of younger girls and missed no opportunity of correcting the etiquette of pretty young flirts. Every dress was too long or too short, too tight or too loose, the wrong color, an ugly tasteless pattern—unless you wore exactly what she did, this spiteful shrew found you in the wrong. If you did wear what she did then you were also in the wrong for trying to show her up.

The other girls in the palace were no better. This one spread malicious rumors about any girl she thought was prettier so that her perceived rivals would not have an advantage in the constant competition for husbands. There was one recently arrived young girl from Tyre who turned all the boys' heads with her thick black hair and black eyes and her alluring foreign-accented Greek. The vicious gossip-monger pretended to be her friend, but started whispering to the handsome boys that she had been sent to Knossos because of a scandal back home: an affair with a married man, a hushed up pregnancy, a miscarriage purposefully induced by imbibing sickening potions brewed by priestesses of strange baby-eating Phoenician gods. The gossip's lying words were believed because she had made herself the confidante of the innocent newcomer. The boys who had once swarmed around the foreign girl, to the point that she would sigh about how hard it was to deal with so many male admirers, now avoided her.

None of her beaus would explain their sudden change of heart. The poor girl became convinced her looks had faded in some inexplicable way. She cried to her secret enemy, whom she still considered to be her dearest friend. The gossip-monger held her and told her to change her style of dress and her makeup in ways that did not flatter her, but made everything worse. The boys were pained at first in feeling the need to shun such a tempting girl. When she began to resemble their doughty mothers, the boys' occasional furtive stares, which the increasingly isolated girl clung to as the last proof of her loveliness, of which she had been so proud, faded away, and the girl found herself alone and neglected. After a barrage of heartfelt, begging letters, her family summoned her home.

The other girls, Ariadne complained to the monster again and again, pretended to be your friends, but always said mean things about you behind your back. It hurt. She wanted to be friends with other girls. She felt that the girls should stick together and try to help each other. They would all wind up stuck with some husband anyhow, probably chosen by some male relative for his own selfish reasons; and the husband would sooner or later become fat, gross, and boring. So they may as well support each other and be kind to one another. But no, each girl was convinced she alone would find that perfect husband: rich, beautiful, wise, loyal, a soldier and hunter with hard, thick muscles with a sympathetic soul able to listen to and soothe his beloved's most secret yearnings—yearnings he could intuit without her speaking them, because he, that special perfect he, would know, somehow just know, what the woman he had married and truly loved was thinking and feeling. And he would know just the right word and caress to make always make anything better. And he would age well. He would keep his gorgeous muscular frame well into middle age. His features would slide seamlessly from youthful beauty to a mature handsomeness. He would be a kind, loving but stern father to their many children. His wife's every day would be bliss.

To land this magic he—whom each girl incarnated in some arrogant prancing young bachelor or other, even though these boys did little but get drunk, wrestle, and mutilate animals in the forest—these other girls would debase themselves freely. They sabotaged each other without stop: here a stained dress, there a smashed perfume bottle, perhaps a subtly placed hint that a particular young lady smiled too often at a muscle-bound sailor or covered up some blemish in her family's history.

Sometimes a group of girls would gang up on a weaker girl. A new girl had come to the palace from the countryside. She was not pretty, and had an unfashionably fat body, which no amount of physician supervised dieting could seem to thin. Nevertheless, her parents needed to marry her off, so they decided to have her try her luck among the noble young men who swarmed about Knossos. They let it be known that this girl, while not a beauty, was the sole heir to the family estates and came with a substantial dowry.

Some of the girls in the palace seethed at the news of this new arrival. These girls had dieted and primped and flirted with ruthless dedication, but were now livid at the thought that the farm hog—as they called her—would get the prize boys through her parents' money. These girls taunted the farm hog miserably—her fat body made every dress hang badly, she was scolded every time she looked at food, she was greeted with mock pig grunts when she walked by.

This cruelty took its toll on the poor girl. She knew she was not pretty, but no one had ever treated her this way. She pined for home. She approached Ariadne and confided in her, hoping that Ariadne would perhaps comfort her. Ariadne did feel bad for the poor unfortunate creature, but really, she was too fat for the beautiful society at the Knossos court, and if the pretty girls saw Ariadne defending the hog, then they would turn their insults upon Ariadne too. Ariadne had no choice but to join in the campaign against the country girl. She even told the clique of pretty tormenters about the girl's secret love of a particular boy, which she had foolishly confided to Ariadne. This led one of the prettiest girls to flirt shamelessly with the boy in question so that he would not notice or speak to any other girls. With this betrayal Ariadne won, for the time being, a reprieve from the cruelty of these other girls. Ariadne knew it was wrong to betray the silly girl who had confided in her, but she sensed she had no choice.

Ariadne hated it all, hated them and their petty scheming, especially as she felt herself forced to join in. She was so glad the monster was such a good and patient listener. She hoped all this girlish blabber did not bore him. Even if he was, well, how to put it ... different ... he was still a boy and must like boy things and not girl gossip. Right, he must like boy things like lobbing spears into the hide of a deer.

The Minotaur looked down. He mumbled a bit embarrassed; he liked hearing about the people in the palace he was not allowed to meet.

Nevertheless, Ariadne wounded the poor monster who still could not tear himself away from her long brown hair and swaying hips. It all started with a visiting Egyptian noble. He was betrothed already to an Egyptian lady. He was in Knossos on a diplomatic mission. The Egyptians were planning to attack some Phoenician cities, or were thinking about such a possible attack, and the Egyptian Pharaoh wanted to make sure Crete stayed neutral in the conflict.

Ariadne was smitten. The monster spent several nights hearing about the young man's deep luscious black eyes and long lashes. And his phy-sique—just the right mixture of beautiful youth and muscular man. He would ride almost naked to the forest to hunt, an eccentricity that comes from growing up in hot deserts, Ariadne thought, and she would longingly watch his exposed upper body tense and turn gracefully on horseback.

At official court functions she would gaze at him as long as she could without making a spectacle of her affections. He was so charming he melted everyone's defenses. Even King Minos seemed friendly to him, at least sometimes. Ariadne would lock eyes with him across the room. These were just fleeting instances, but she was absolutely certain she knew, in those moments, their souls connected. He saw her yearning and despair and was giving her hope. But it was hopeless. He was engaged. He was a for-eigner from an alien place. He could not speak Greek very well. He contin-ually said things in his strange guttural language to the Egyptian ambassador who would translate them into passable Greek. There was no point in this silly game.

Or maybe there was a chance? What if she sent him a note? Confessed her true feelings? Maybe he was waiting for her to give a sign. Maybe she only needed to send the right signal and they would elope. Far away. To Babylon. Yes, great, bustling Babylon where they could marry and lead a new life. What did the Minotaur think?

The monster had never felt such a horrible pain. His stomach knotted tightly at her twittering words. He wanted to cry. Or to take this Egyptian and rip his arms out of their sockets. With a concerted effort, the Minotaur kept his composure. He gave the obvious advice, which Ariadne expected and likely was trying to elicit: The foreign diplomat is engaged to one of his own, no doubt after delicate negotiations. Leave him be, do not let yourself get hurt chasing a man you can never have. Ariadne nodded. She knew this was true and merely needed to hear it said out loud. She squeezed the monster's hands and walked away, the breeze blowing her light dress and her hips slightly swaying. The monster's eyes followed her meandering stroll back to her apartment in the palace.

The Egyptian left soon enough. But then there were others. It seemed Ariadne found true love and heartbreak on each new half moon.

There was the young Cretan lord with the curly blond hair, a champion javelin thrower. She had watched him train and loved his tight, lean body as it glided gracefully in the gymnasium. She had thought he was attracted to her at the recent festival banquet, but then he pretended to go home early. Ariadne followed and spied on him, not in a malicious way, but she was worried about him. He had seemed a little drunk. However, in the courtyard of his family's villa, she saw him kissing another girl. Boys were such liars. Why couldn't they just say when they wanted another girl more? The monster offered her reassuring words and tried to hide his discomfort. He was angry and at the same time he felt embarrassed about being angry.

The treacherous javelin thrower was followed by a prince from Pylos on the Greek mainland. This prince had dark blue eyes and long black curls. Ariadne swooned and swore she could look into those eyes forever. She tried flirting with him. She would go up to him, praise his strength, and ask him about Pylos. She told him how gorgeous his eyes were. At first the young prince politely volleyed conversation with her, but he soon grew weary of Ariadne's attentions. She could tell she was boring him so she tried every trick she knew to engage him—she played with his fingers, tossed her hair, let her dress slip over so her leg was revealed, as if by accident—but all to no avail. He finally dismissed her one afternoon with an insult about the puny size of her breasts. Did the Minotaur think her breasts were too small? Did all boys want really big ones? She was beautiful, the monster told her, any man could see that. She smiled and squeezed his hand, and sauntered off with her swaying gait. The monster hurt, but felt trapped by the rhythm of her legs and hips.

The Minotaur was jealous of all these men. Yet he also hated them for rejecting Ariadne, even though in his jealousy he did not want them to be Ariadne's lovers. The monster could not keep his emotions straight, and felt angry at himself.

On the other hand, these talks with Ariadne were still somehow exhilarating and would leave the monster dizzy with desire. Ariadne was so close to him. She sat right next to him, and her leg, which she swung about when her words raced, would graze the monster's legs. She confided in him and trusted him, more than anyone else in Knossos, certainly more than the vain, cruel boys of the palace court. The monster thought she saw through his frightening bull's head and horrible jagged horns and knew he was a good, kind gentle soul, the one who could best love her and care for her.

The monster knew that he could love Ariadne truly, not like these spoiled fickle boys who played with girls in between bloodthirsty hunting expeditions. He could be the husband who would make her happy. The two of them would leave this hideous palace—more a prison than a castle—and move back to Ariadne's country estate. The Minotaur imagined he would work on a farm or a vineyard, and labor with other men at simple, honest work. The other men would be scared of him at first, but they would soon learn he was no monster in his soul, despite his horrifying appearance.

Thus was born the monster's plan: He would declare himself to Ariadne and propose marriage to her. The Minotaur rehearsed his speech over and over again in his mind, rehearsed his arguments and her hesitant responses and his powerful rejoinders, which would win her over. The monster would explain he had seen the beauty of her soul and he knew she had seen the beauty of his soul. Conniving, plotting Knossos court life was no place for two such tender spirits that prized true love and not cunning or physical beauty or glory or wealth. The monster plotted the couple's daring escape from the palace to Ariadne's country estates, and how he would send word to his mother of their elopement. Maybe his mother would realize how rotten life was at the palace and would move her household to the countryside, too. The monster thought she would delight in rocking grandchildren to sleep on the veranda of the family villa.

During the course of the succeeding nights the monster tried to find a time and an opening to make his grand speech. But it was hard to find the right moment of comfortable quiet in which the monster could begin; Ariadne's rapid fire monologues rushed from her tongue without pause. The Minotaur fidgeted with the stones on the ground and drew in the dirt with his big toe. His leg shook unconsciously and violently. The monster's attention would wander and he found that Ariadne's voice would many times dissolve into a steady humming and buzzing pounding on his head. Ariadne, though, did not notice the monster's discomfort, or, at least, did not mention it or ask about it. She barreled on as before, consumed by her own petty world.

Finally, one night, as Ariadne was about to begin her usual barrage, the monster found his courage:

Ariadne, wait, please. I have something to tell you. It is important.

She stopped and looked confused and a bit wary. Her body moved slightly away from the Minotaur. She said nothing.

Ariadne, you are the sweetest, most kind, wonderful, beautiful, noble girl in Crete, in all of Hellas. I hate the way the young noblemen and the ladies at court treat you. You deserve so much better. You are better than them. They cannot understand a gentle, kind, loving creature like you.

I want you to be happy. So much I want you to be happy.

Ariadne's back had straightened, tightly. Her body was tense. Her eyes were alert and fixed on the monster's face.

Ariadne, I know that I am not what you imagined as a husband, but I love and appreciate you, and I can make you happy. You pour your heart out to me because I am the one who really understands you. Let's leave this place with its wretched petty intrigues and jealousies. Let's elope and run off to your estate, in the country, where there are other kind, good souls like us. We can work the farm and vineyards together. I know we can be so happy if we just get away from all these people here in Knossos. Please, Ariadne, will you give me your hand in marriage?

Ariadne stood up and jumped back in one motion. Her face was a mix of horror and disgust. The monster stayed seated on the bench. He could not move or speak. He looked down at the dirt around his feet.

Ariadne stared at the monster, her body rigid and tense, pondering what to say. And it was then that the terrible, grotesque change came over her: her muscles relaxed, her breathing slowed, her hands unclenched, and a smile crept over her face.

Ariadne laughed. She laughed slowly at first, but as she thought further about the silliness of a hideous monster in love, pleading for her hand, of the terrible scary beast crying his heart out, she laughed harder and longer and louder, so loudly that she covered her mouth to avoid drawing attention or waking anyone. She tried to speak, but she could not get any words out of her mouth. The laughter erupted uncontrollably within her, and she could do nothing but give in. This is cruel, Ariadne thought; but I can't help myself, it's so funny. He looks so ridiculous with his pouting bull-mouth and begging horns.

The monster burrowed his gaze further into the dirt and pebbles at his feet. He said nothing and did not move. He gripped the side of the bench tightly with his hands.

At some point that evening Ariadne walked away, still laughing out loud and shaking her head. The Minotaur did not watch her walk away, but kept his eyes down. He listened to the laughter and waited for it to fade into the darkness.

IV. The Monster Seeks to Change His Fate

THE MONSTER WOULD never be able to recall how or when he came home that night, but somehow, and sometime, he made it back to his bed chamber. Once under his blankets, he could not bring himself to get up again. His soul was stripped of all desire: food, drink, exercise, gardens, scrolls and stories—none of it seemed worth the effort of moving his heavy, clunky body. The longer the monster lay down in his open-eyed stupor, the further he slipped into a state between waking and dreaming: too tired to be awake, but too awake to sleep. He stared up at his ceiling full of painted stars, but could no longer make out the constellations. The stars had lost their order and become a jumbled mess of dots tossed against the ceiling.

But worst of all was the hideous laughter of Ariadne. Her cackle would echo in the room; the monster would cover his ears with his pillow, but that only served to muffle every sound but the loud laugh. The laugh seemed to have taken on a life of its own. He could barely recall Ariadne's face and form, and he could not summon in his mind the image of her face laughing. Yet the laugh itself seemed to have broken free of its mistress and to have taken up residence in the Minotaur's bed chamber. He cursed it, but was helpless to exorcise it.

The monster reflected that there were two kinds of tales: the ones in scrolls and the ones told by his beloved, senile yaya. Tales in scrolls were serious: The stakes were high for the earnest heroes and princesses and gods, and a failure of heart meant death or betrayal. The whole confrontation between hero and enemy—whether monster, god, or evil king,—was told in a fever pitch with no room for laughs. To laugh at a hero battling desperately for his beloved or his people was absolutely unacceptable, if not immoral—that would be like laughing at a funeral procession.

Then the monster considered the tales of his yaya. Those tales were all about laughter. The deadly seriousness of the hero's quest was always collapsing amid a series of toothaches, stomach cramps, belches, poor hygiene, and ludicrous misunderstandings—like a hero who had never seen a fig and thought it was a little green monster ready to kill him upon waking. In these stories the stakes were low: Monsters always turned out to be harmless and scared, loves were exaggerated and silly, and no one really could be hurt or would suffer.

The Minotaur had always thought of himself as one of the characters in the tales told in the scrolls. But now his room was haunted by a cackling, laughing ghost that could only be born from the rollicking humor of Yaya's earthy, deprecating lore. The monster could not expel the farce story spirit who, he was certain, did not belong with him. Sometimes he would think it was gone, feel his half-awake mind drift towards heroic deeds, only to be assaulted at the most dramatic moments by Ariadne's stifled laugh gently gurgling in his ear.

Queen Pasiphae could not hear the wicked laughter spirit. However, she drew her own conclusion about why her son was moaning in bed: All those nighttime excursions had led him to catch a terrible chill. She promptly marshaled her medical battalions to battle this illness. Her personal physician was summoned, examined the patient, and prescribed all sorts of orange-brown, viscous medicines, which the monster found difficult to swallow. Furthermore, the medicines gave him genuine stomach cramps. Doubled over in pain from these potions, the monster was doted on by his mother, the queen, who gave him plentiful helpings of water and grass, which actually did restore the Minotaur's strength and spirits.

The medicinal siege finally compelled the monster to get up. If nothing else, he knew, absent some positive sign of healthiness, he would have more orange-brown draughts to swallow, no doubt followed by ever greater cramps. The fussing and the potions also distracted his ears from the sound of the cackling ghost of Ariadne's laughter. It was still there, faintly humming in the background, but the Minotaur was pleased to discover it could be drowned out, at least sometimes.

It took a couple of days for the monster to return to a regular pattern of waking and sleeping. Previously, his excitement at seeing Ariadne had been so great that he shook with energy all through the garden nights and collapsed into happy, tingling exhaustion at dawn. It took some time for his body to adjust to the loss of the excitement his beloved had given him. The Minotaur worried he would never again feel anything but tired and bored. However, after a few nights in which he actually slept, and a few days of good eating (the cook tried to cheer him with wonderfully spiced leaf salads) he was restored to a more regular level of alertness.

But still, the laughing demon spirit followed him, hounded him, everywhere he went. It would echo in the sound of the wind shaking the branches of the fig tree in the window of his bed chamber and in the sound of the wine being poured into his cup. Unable to escape the laughter, the monster began to listen closely to it. In the beginning, it was simply cruel and contemptuous, note after note. So he listened more closely. Then one day it happened. The Minotaur heard the message in the laugh: You have no destiny, you have no future, you can make no plans. Monsters like you float in the present—until you are cut down by the appropriate hero. You do not get married and live to old age.

The monster tried to drown out the laughing ghost again. This time he buried himself in his scrolls. He read the tale of Actaeon, the great hunter. Actaeon went with his well-trained hunting dogs deep into the thick wood, pursuing ever greater and mightier game. He pressed hard. He went deeper into the forest than human men were supposed to go, and as a consequence saw something that he was not permitted to see—the beautiful goddess Artemis naked and bathing in a lake in a clearing in the forest. He was captivated; he stood gaping at the goddess's perfect, athletic, dripping wet body. She saw him. Artemis did not laugh; this was not a tale with laughter. She was furious and ashamed. In her rage she cursed Actaeon and turned him into a deer. He ran away. But his hunting dogs, not recognizing their master in his beastly form, took him for prey, and true to his own training lessons tore his limbs to pieces and feasted on his body.

The tale fascinated the still reeling monster: a slight turn of the goddess's magic, prompted by a moment's unreflecting rage, changed Actaeon's fate from the hunter to the hunted. A change in form meant a change in fate. For those like Actaeon blessed with a beautiful, limber form, a form fashioned for strength and domination, the change of form meant tragedy. For Actaeon, to be transformed was to be cursed.

But what about my lot, thought the Minotaur. He considered his own form to be cursed, and the cackling, riotous laughter heartily agreed. He was born stricken with the curse of a monster bull's head and a monster bull's horns. What if he could remove his curse? What if, the monster thought, he could engineer Artemis's spell in reverse—transform the beast into the beautiful, fully human Actaeon? The monster reasoned that if he could exchange his terrifying, menacing bull's head for a noble, lovely human head, one like those atop the young men who made Ariadne swoon at banquets, then his fate would be transformed, too.

The Minotaur's imagination swam with excitement. One look from a beautiful human face, a new face, would slay the laughing spirit once and for all. Ariadne would see a beauty of body to match his beauty of soul, and she would be helpless to resist his charms. They would marry this time. He would generously accept her heartfelt apology for her thoughtless and hurtful behavior in the past. The newlyweds would leave the palace and make a household together on Ariadne's country estate. They would have beautiful children who would be the spitting image of their beautiful father. The reversal of the curse would be passed on to the next generation, and to the generation after—a dynasty of rustic beauties would be born.

So all the monster had to do was find a way to work the necessary magic. Unfortunately, this was something beyond what he could discern from a close reading of the scrolls, even esoteric scrolls lodged in the libraries of ancient temples. He could not count on the assistance of any god. Being stuck in the queen's tower had deprived him of the opportunity to offer sacrifices and speak to oracles, which were the well-established paths of currying divine favor. What the Minotaur needed, he concluded, was a friendly witch.

But how to find one? Witches certainly swarmed, discreetly, throughout Knossos and the countryside, performing services for the ill and the lovesick. Yet they were not in residence in the queen's tower. The monster would need to find a way to summon a witch from the outside. This would involve surmounting two hurdles: finding someone to confide in and finding a convincing reason for why he needed a witch. The monster did not believe anyone would take his lovesickness seriously. Their laughter would simply join the chorus of echoing, harsh laughs let loose upon him by Ariadne.

While stuck in this conundrum, fate intervened to help him—or so the monster believed. He was sitting in the kitchen on a lazy, humid summer afternoon. He was eating a late lunch. The cook had prepared for him a wondrous salad of grass, leaves, and figs, soaked in honey. The cook gave the Minotaur warm milk with honey to pair with the sweet salad. As always, the monster's ears were searching for some other sound to drown out Ariadne's persistent, haunting laughter. At that meal, his ears found the cook's conversation, on the other side of the kitchen, with a young servant girl. The cook was in the middle of a story, her voice growing both louder and faster:

I am telling you, dear, it is all true. I saw it myself. One day she was the ugliest girl in Knossos. Poor creature grew up in filth in a back alley. Bent back, warts everywhere, some of those warts with twisting, greasy hairs growing from them, she was the ugliest girl you have ever seen. She was young, real young, but she would have lost a beauty contest to the most wrinkled old maid. You would think some girl that ugly and poor would set her sights suitably low when it came to a husband, and be grateful for whatever she got. Not that one, no, she lost her heart to one of King Minos's guards. And not just any old guard—as if she would have stood a chance with any one of them—but a young man with a broad chest and tight blonde curls and a lovely face with these blue eyes that just melted your heart when he looked at you. That was the husband that little Miss Hairy Warts from the filth pile decided to make her own.

Still, the girl was no dummy. She knew she had to do something about her appearance. She was not going to have a chance with this fellow unless she could go from smelly ogre to beauty. How would she pull that trick off?

She decided to become a witch. But you had to hand it to a humble, low born girl, she put on no airs. She started as an apprentice. Miss Wart Face went to every witch in town, begging to serve them if they would take her on as an apprentice. There were a lot of slammed doors and shoves to the dirt. But she finally got one to take her on. Not that it was easy work. Witch's apprentices are the ones sent to find dead rats or graveyard dirt. Sometimes they have to steal objects needed for their mistresses' spells and concoctions. Many times Wart Face barely escaped arrest, and then only to go home to a scolding by her mistress because she got some little thing wrong. Still, she worked hard, and she paid close attention to those spells. She studied hard.

After a couple of years, she had what she needed: a spell to make her beautiful and, if that was not enough, a recipe for a love potion to ensnare Mr. Dreamy Big Blue Eyes from King Minos's guards. Miss Wart Face's mistress lived across from my sister in the same courtyard. You know my sister, the one married to the cobbler who drinks away his money, the rotten bastard. One day, I was visiting my sister and she and her drunken cobbler husband start going at it, and I mean really going at it. Yelling, cursing, throwing plates and pans at each other. Their little daughter was frightened out of her precious little mind. So I said, sweetie, come outside, come take a walk with your auntie, it is a pretty night.

When we went outside what did we see, Miss Wart Face, in a corner in the courtyard, by herself, with a big fire going, blazing and roaring. She was throwing things in the fire, don't ask me what. The fire lit up her ugly face so it was the only part of her you could see in the darkness. I swear, the warts had grown bigger and had married each other and made baby warts together on her face. She looked worse than ever. There was something crazy in her eyes. She didn't notice us, or anything. She just kept looking at her fire, throwing things into it, mumbling her crazy mumbo-jumbo witch talk. I know I should have gone away, nothing good happens when you go eavesdropping on a witch, but I couldn't help myself. It seemed like something big was going to happen.

Let me tell you, was I ever right and how. After howling and hissing and tossing and waving her arms about the fire for who knows how long, Miss Wart Face suddenly stopped. She became totally silent. She did not move at all, not one tiny bit. She just looked into the fire with that crazy look in her eyes. And then it happened. The warts melted off her face, her back straightened. She grew real tall, like our lady, the queen. Her face became like that of a princess, and her greasy, patchy black hair became long, thick, and red. She put out the fire, this huge bonfire, with one quick breath, like it was a baby candle. Miss Wart Face was now the Red Princess. And that Red Princess married her guard, with his big muscles and blue eyes, a couple of months later. He apparently fell head over heels the moment he laid eyes on her new body and face.

You think she would be satisfied, but no, not her. Our Red Princess then discovered that King Minos did not pay the infantry like lords. Her gallant dreamboat was easy on the eyes, but lived in an even more cramped room than hers, and in a much more squalid courtyard. Well, the Red Princess would have none of that. She had not done all that work so her new beautiful skin could roll in dirt and soot. So she set up shop as an elegant witch for elegant ladies. No more strange, smelly, mumbling, toothless little old crones who were so embarrassing for your fancy merchants' wives. No, they all began to hire the Red Princess as their witch. She came to their fancy big villas, they sipped wine in crystal glasses and ate olives on the porches. Then she would do a bit of witchery to snuff out some worry or other. And did they ever pay the Red Princess well. She made so much money she soon had her own big fancy villa with a fine porch for wine-drinking and olive-eating. She told her lovely husband to quit his job—she was terrified some drunken brawl would lead to a scar on his beautiful flesh. After all she did to get her hands on those lovely white muscles, there was no way she was letting him blemish them in any way. She put him under some kind of spell so that he would stay forever young and beautiful. But also, he could not leave the house without her. He is more like a pet than a husband. He even stopped wanting to go hunting with his friends in the palace guards, if you could believe it.

Some girls have all the luck, I guess. I will probably die here, leaning over this stove, trying to decide which of my calluses is the most flattering to my complexion.

The cook sighed. She stared at her big, weathered, pockmarked hands. The young servant girl consoled her: Auntie, don't be sad, it will work out for you. You will see, Eros will shoot an arrow straight at some nice man, and he will marry you and take you away from here.

The cook silently turned her head and frowned. The servant girl looked down and stopped talking.

That night the Minotaur dreamed of the Red Princess. He saw himself approach her in a sun drenched villa in the early morning. She was wearing a flowing red dress that fluttered slightly. She was tall and erect; her hands were clasped together in front of her torso. She had kind eyes. She said to the Minotaur that she understood the heartbreak of being a monster. She would save him, as she had saved herself, and he would win his beloved, just as she had won her beloved. She was the good witch who would free all unjustly cursed monsters and make them beautiful.

The monster awoke with a startled, excited jump. He saw what he needed to do. He delayed his breakfast until after his mother and her servants had eaten. When he was sure they had all finished eating, he went downstairs to the kitchen. He was, as he had hoped, alone with the cook. She served him the breakfast she had prepared. He ate; she cleaned the dishes used by the other breakfasters and hummed a tune he did not recognize.

The monster breathed hard and rehearsed his words in his mind. Then he spoke, focusing his mind on projecting a relaxed tone:

Auntie, I could not help overhearing your story yesterday about the Red Princess. Was that all true?

You better believe it. Every word.

Does the Red Princess live in Knossos still? Do you know her?

Yes, I still know her. She doesn't like to talk to people who knew her when she was the Wart Princess, but she talks to me because every once in a while I can help get one of her clients into a reception with the queen. Those fancy merchants' wives love your mother. They act like she is some kind of goddess. I keep saying listen, trust me, she eats lamb and picks her teeth like any other woman, no one knows better than me, but they don't listen.

Auntie, I need to ask you a favor. About the Red Princess.

What silly notions do you have cooking in those thick silly horns on your end? Why would you want to talk to her?

I need a witch, Auntie. My sickness—remember when I could not get up from my blankets—well, it is back. And worse. The doctor's medicines only made it worse last time. I am scared to tell my mother. She will just summon more physicians with more potions that do not work and make me sicker. But the Red Princess, perhaps she has a cure? And if she cures Queen Pasiphae's son, won't my mother really be in her debt? Lots of invitations for merchants' wives. Please, Auntie, please help me. I can't drink those awful medicines again.

The cook stopped her work and looked over towards the monster. His big bull eyes were bent forward, fixated on her, hopefully. She sighed and bit her lower lip. She looked down and then back at those big eyes.

Fine, the cook said, but it will not be easy to smuggle her in. It will have to be late at night. I will give you word beforehand. You will have to spend the night where I tell you to in the tower.

The Minotaur smiled broadly and thanked her profusely.

Thus began the waiting. At each meal of each day the monster would wait for a message. He began to eat extra meals and was always early to mealtime now. He would stare at the cook and watch her for some sign, paying no attention anymore to the pretty young servant girls. When the monster realized the cook was actively squirming under his stare, and that the servant girls were giggling about a wedding match between the old cook and the Minotaur, he reined himself in. He adopted a practice of staring at his plate, counting to three hundred, looking up at the cook, counting to ten, and then staring back down at his plate to commence a new count to three hundred. This numerical discipline soothed the monster and eased the anxious but slow passage of time.

Still, the waiting was hard and took its toll. The monster was beginning to lose heart, and he thought that all these counting games were just so much silly childish nonsense. One night, though, the cook whispered into his ear at dinner: Tonight. Slip out of your bedchamber and to the kitchen. She will meet you here.

The monster nodded and tried to suppress his excitement. He did not want to draw attention to himself or arouse suspicion. Worried he would give himself away, or be tempted to ask a question too many and so try the goodwill of the cook, the monster retired early to his bed chamber. His big hulking body paced around and around the small room. His fantasies ran riot: marriage to Ariadne, picnics with their children in the countryside, working with lovely Ariadne to fix up an old abandoned cottage, which sat—and why not?—next to a clear lake with little golden fish and soaring birds.

Once the sun had set, and the dinner table was cleared of the last evening meal, the monster slipped from his room into a corner of the kitchen. He could not sleep anyway. He shook his leg as quietly as he could to release his pent up energy. The Minotaur played little mental games to distract himself: he counted the floor tiles by the moonlight, or tried to debate whether he wanted his new human head to have dark hair or blonde hair. Or would the spell not allow him to choose, he wondered. Perhaps he could only be one kind of human. But he hoped that he could choose—at least some small feature, like eye color. He wanted sea green eyes.

Two shadows wrapped in long brown cloaks slipped into the dark kitchen with swift, hushed steps. The monster recognized the smaller, squat shadow as the cook. Next to her was a tall slender figure—so tall that the figure, which was hooded, bent its head to avoid hitting the ceiling. The cook lit a small candle on the table where the Minotaur was sitting and then shuffled silently back to the door frame. The dim yellow flame lit up the monster's bull head and long, sharp horns, but little else.

The tall figure recoiled and flinched upon seeing the Minotaur's face. But then the tall figure walked slowly to the table. The tall figure stood over the monster and reached out a long finger crowned by a long and blood-red painted nail and, ever so slightly, touched the side of one of his horns. Encouraged by the monster's apparent docility, the finger explored further, feeling hide, ears, and then the human chest and arms. The monster could not move or speak. He watched the movements of that finger, and admired the blood hued paint on the nail, which was further dotted with small glittery sparkles, like miniature stars drifting about his body. The feel of the nail on his skin was cold and hard, and the monster felt strangely in danger when the nail slid up and down his chest. The nail was too confident of its power over the flesh that it grazed.

Once the nail completed its inspection, the finger retreated back into the long cloak. The tall figure moved next to the Minotaur and, from under the thick hood, looked down upon him. Then the tall figure took the seat next to his and pulled off of its hood. The face that was revealed had olive skin without a blemish. Her hair was bright red and piled up in a large bobbing bun atop her head. Her face was a slender oval, framed by two reptile green eyes and a long, slim nose. The two looked at each other. The Minotaur still could not speak. He was looking for the traces of warts on her skin, but could find none. She had shed her monster hide without so much as the smallest hint remaining, he mused. The thought cheered him, but not enough to give him the courage to speak.

The Red Princess leaned forward. She offered a forced, but ingratiating half smile. She spoke in a soft tone:

Young Prince, you know who I am. I have answered your summons. I am here to help you. I am devoted to your mother, our great Queen Pasiphae. Please, tell me what ails you. I can help. Do not be nervous.

The slight smile and the honeyed tones made the monster's head dizzy with nervousness and delight. Then he recalled that, in fact, he had made the summons of this woman and this was his chance to be transformed into the beautiful man he was meant to be. He steeled himself:

Wise and learned woman, mistress of secret knowledge, I have come to you with a delicate matter. I wish to change my fate. I have the soul of a noble hero, with a great abundance of love in his heart. I am not meant to suffer the fate of a monster. I do not want to be a monster. I don't want to terrorize anyone, and I don't want to be hunted. Please, I beg you, free me from this curse. I have no doubt that my mother, the queen, will be forever in your debt if you can transform her son from monster to handsome prince.

The Red Princess turned her head slightly to the side and squinted. She tapped her fingers lightly and scrunched up her face, as if concentrating hard on some difficult problem.

I can help you. I can make you a man. A handsome, strapping man, in fact. Give me three days. I will prepare the necessary mixture for you to drink. I will have it sent to your cook, with instructions. Follow them exactly; this is a tricky spell, it must be calibrated just right. I ask no payment except your word to ask Queen Pasiphae to look kindly upon me.

The monster's body collapsed from tension to relaxation. He slumped forward towards the table and smiled in one simultaneous motion. Thank you, thank you, he whispered. He looked at her, but he made no additional movement. He waited for the witch's direction.

The Red Princess smiled again, broader this time, kindly and indulgently. She slowly stood. She placed the hood back over her head in an unhurried gesture. She reached a hand out from under the cloak and used all five fingers to caress the Minotaur's rough cheek hides. Again he watched the explosion of sparkles dancing from her long blood-colored nails. Soon she removed her hand from the monster, and the cook escorted her out. The cook also signaled to the Minotaur to leave the kitchen. He stood, blew the light out in one try, and walked back to his bed chamber.

His spirit was light that evening. The monster looked up at the painting of the stars on his ceiling, lit by the moon shining through his window. He no longer tried to find the constellations, but rather saw the stars as painted sparkles on an infinite array of beautiful painted nails on long, slender feminine fingers. These nails gently stroked his head and sang him a lullaby with their tender, circling caresses.

Once more, the monster was forced to wait and to guard his secret machinations. He paced back and forth in his room over and over again. With a new sense of hope he would peek out of his window into the palace gardens, hoping to see Ariadne again. He strained his eyes, and tried different times of the day and the night, but he could see nothing except strangers strolling. Some of these strangers were young men, nobles, flirting with coy but teasing girls. The monster tried to discern which of these boys he would soon look like; he decided then that he wanted thick, wavy blonde hair and brown eyes (instead of green), in a rectangular face. He wanted a small forehead and a low hairline, like the young braggart leaning over a girl at that moment in the far pavilion. Although he could not see Ariadne, the monster was dizzy from admiring all the different young girls milling about the gardens. While Ariadne was his true love, whom he would always prefer, the Minotaur was nevertheless pleased that handsome young men appeared to have many lovely girls to choose from. He would soon himself be able to sample all of these girls, although of course he would still somehow always remain true only to Ariadne.

The monster was certain the end of his heartache was at hand. The ghost of Ariadne's sneering laugh had vanished, embarrassed and ashamed in front of the Minotaur's soon to be new human head. The monster walked about the queen's tower with energy and confidence. He ate his meals with gusto and joy, and even asked for second helpings. He whistled and hummed as he walked about the queen's tower, and winked mischievously at the younger servant girls, who would drop their baskets in surprise, embarrassment, or, if the girl were new, fright. The monster's feet seemed to dance in the hallways and stairways, and he was always rushing to volunteer with the carrying or lifting of this or that heavy bag or pile of wood. He felt expansive and generous towards what he now felt was a good world, which would soon be his playground.

The servants gossiped about what had gotten into the monster prince. Queen Pasiphae assumed that her physicians' elixirs had worked their healing power, and made a note to reward her personal physician with new and greater privileges. Others assumed he had secretly found a sweetheart, maybe a girl monster hidden somewhere in the palace. There were several hushed debates about whether two monsters could make a monster baby ....

The cook, however, kept her silence. The cook watched the bounding monster with a wary eye. She seemed worried. She said nothing, but she continually frowned as she watched the Minotaur. When the monster was absent, her eyes seemed to stray to a far distant point and she did not listen to the conversations humming about her. The cook was sometimes seen mumbling to herself. But the members of the queen's household took little notice, as the sudden turnaround in the monster's spirits was the topic of all the gossip in the queen's tower.

When the third day came, the cook discreetly requested an afternoon off from her duties, as, she explained, her niece was ill and she owed a visit. The queen readily agreed. The monster watched her walk down the stairs, his leg shaking rapidly without him realizing it. He was sure that his hour of deliverance had come. He reflected that his life up until then had been an unhappy dream, a grotesque nightmare, from which he was about to awake. The monster felt his real life was at last set to begin, and he could step out of his absurd monster costume and into his true body.

The afternoon and the early evening were excruciating for the monster. Excitement gave way to impatience, and impatient thoughts about why the cook was taking so long in turn birthed anxious, fearful thoughts about everything that could go wrong: either the cook or the Red Princess decided to drop their plan to help him; or the Red Princess decided to demand an exorbitant payment; or an ingredient was missing; or some fool priest attacked the Red Princess for sacrilegious conduct. The "ors" went on and on in the Minotaur's mind, circling in a mad screaming frenzy and gave him no peace.

The monster's tension was only relieved late that night. He was lying in a corner in the kitchen. He had tried to stay awake to greet the cook upon her return, but his overwrought nerves and dizzying, nail-biting worries had sapped his strength, and he had collapsed into slumber without intending to. Now, he felt a rough, callused hand shake his shoulder violently. The Minotaur woke with a start. He looked up and saw, dimly, the outline of the cook's body. It was late at night, and the room was dark. Black clouds were pouring rain down thickly upon Knossos and blocking the light of the moon and the stars. There was a wet, lapping breeze from the window, which made him shiver. He was not sure how long he had slept.

The cook walked over to the kitchen table where she had placed two objects. The first was lit, a round candle, which gave off an orange light and illuminated about half of the table. The monster could not make out what the other object was—it was too far from the candle's light. The cook said nothing, but moved her hand forcefully through the air in a waving motion to signal to the monster to come join her at the table.

The Minotaur rose with some difficulty. Sleeping on the floor had hurt his neck and back, and his body was stiff. After laboriously straitening himself, the monster walked haltingly to the table. Much to his own surprise he felt his steps to be heavy and his feet to be weighed down by some enigmatic force. Still, by fits and starts he made it to the table and sat down in the faint glow of the candlelight. The cook dove straight to the point:

Here is the potion. From her.

She moved a jar, the second object on the table, in front of the Minotaur. The jar was unusual: It was neither translucent glass nor thick clay. Instead, the sides and bottom were black in color and smooth to the touch like finely wrought glass. The stopper on top was thick and brown.

No smell escaped the jar. The monster picked the jar up and could tell, from its weight, that something was in it.

The Red Princess gave strict instructions to me, to say to you, about how to use this potion. You need to fast tomorrow. Instead of breakfast, you will drink half the jar. Instead of lunch, you will drink the other half. After you finish the jar you are to lie down and close your eyes firmly. And wait. The potion should do its work as you sleep. To help you sleep, the witch put a sleeping draught in the potion, too.

The Red Princess said you should open the jar and drink only when you are completely alone. In between your breakfast and your lunch, you have to push the stopper back in real tight. When you are done hide the jar somewhere. The witch says she will want this jar back when you are done. I hope this works, but this kind of business makes me nervous. So many things can go wrong with witches and their potions and incantations. Let's hope you do not wake up turned into a fly. If you are some insect, remember I tried to help you and bite the washerwoman instead. She deserves it anyway.

The cook laughed to herself. She stood up, leaned down, and blew out the candle with a swift, forceful breath. She walked briskly away, mumbling and yawning, to get some much needed rest for her taxed nerves.

The monster sat at the table in the dark fondling the strange jar. He could not figure out what it was made of, which started to bother him, although he knew he should not care about the jar. He was curious to examine this potion, perhaps just to sniff it. But then he reflected that strong magic could be delicate and thought better of opening the jar too soon. He twisted the little vessel in his palm in different circular motions for some time. The rain started to pour harder. The kitchen became uncomfortably cold and slightly wet as the wind sent rain in through the narrow window slit. The Minotaur eventually picked up the jar and walked back to his bed chamber.

The monster pulled a small chest out from under his bed. He kept various old jars and bottles there. He gently, and slowly, placed the Red Princess's jar in the chest. He pushed the chest gingerly back under his bed. For a moment he was scared that he had woken his mother. He was relieved when he heard the low growl of her snoring over the pitter patter of the fast moving rain.

The monster lay back and tried to sleep, he squeezed his eyes shut and commanded his body to slumber, but sleep evaded him. He woke again and again in the night, terrified that somehow the chest and its precious load had vanished. He would scramble to his bed and grab the chest from underneath the bed frame. He would open the chest hurriedly—sometimes too hurriedly, and his fingers would fumble about the hinges haphazardly—and fondle again the strange jar. With his worries relieved for that moment, the monster would put the jar back in the chest and the chest back under the bed.

This cycle of worrying, waking, and checking tormented the Minotaur through the entire night. He finally entered a deep sleep around dawn, and he did not wake up until just past his usual breakfast time. Once the monster cleared the film from his eyes and got his bearings, he realized that it was time for his first drink. He rose cautiously and tiptoed to his door. He pushed it ever so slightly ajar and peaked out; he was alone. He closed the door slowly, so as to avoid making any sound.

The monster walked back to his bed and pulled out the chest, opened it, and lifted the jar to his lap. He stared at it for a moment. He hoped its taste would be palatable. He started to pull the stopper off, but then pulled back. For an instant the monster felt paralyzed and imagined everything that could go wrong—maybe the witch botched the potion or mixed her draughts up, and he was about to turn himself into a mosquito. The Minotaur steeled himself: This is your chance, he told his body, no more silly fears. Be a man, drink.

The monster put one hand on the base of the jar and the other on the stopper. Holding the base tightly, he removed the stopper with one firm pull. There was a faint popping sound. This sound was followed by the sickly sweet smell of overripe fruit rotting in a scorching late summer sun. The potion itself had a rusted copper color and thin consistency. Fighting his revulsion at the smell, the Minotaur raised the jar to his mouth, muttered a silent toast to his true and soon to be revealed manhood and drank half the jar. The aftertaste was strong and syrupy, and the monster tried to swallow his saliva to dilute it. He placed the jar down upon a nearby table, grabbed the base firmly, and, after some effort, reinserted the stopper. As instructed, he placed the jar back in the chest, but this time left the chest on the floor of his room.

The monster soon felt drowsy. To his surprise he was not hungry at all. With the strength of his eyelids failing fast, the Minotaur soon fell asleep again. This sleep was dreamless and deep and dark. It was more akin to being drugged than to a healthy rest.

The monster was awakened a few hours later by a bright sun ray burning his closed eyes. The rain clouds had dispersed, and the sun was beating harshly on the wet ground. The Minotaur sat up with effort. Despite the sleep he felt groggy, with heavy, deadened limbs. He felt unable to awake fully, but seemed instead to be trapped in a half-alert haze. The monster saw the position of the sun in the sky and surmised he had slept until lunchtime. He reached over to the chest on the floor with his foot and dragged it over. The monster leaned down, opened the chest, removed the jar, and pulled off the stopper, which again made a faint popping sound. Carefully raising and balancing the jar to his mouth in his numbed state, the Minotaur drank the rest of the potion in one gulp. He lazily tossed both the jar and the stopper separately back into the chest, watching them land interspersed in the jumble of odds and ends in the chest. The monster lacked the energy to straighten up. In his haze, he hoped that nothing broke, but did not bother to check.

The monster tried to raise himself up, but all the sensation in his body was gone. He did not so much fall asleep as feel his life force drain away, leaving nothing left but an exhausted husk without the strength to be alert and awake. This new sleep was again dreamless and almost suffocating. The Minotaur felt imprisoned in his own inability to open his eyes or move his body parts.

The monster awoke the next morning with a pounding headache. He was sure for a moment that the potion had worked: now he was a man, a beautiful man. Everything was fixed and as it should be. He eagerly reached his hand to his face.

But the monster's hand felt his bull's hide and bull's ear and bull's horns. He jumped up and grabbed a small mirror on top of his dresser. Nothing had changed—he looked exactly the same. The magic had failed him.

The Minotaur slumped down upon the bed. He stared at the floor. He thought that he should be angry—perhaps the Red Princess had betrayed him, although he could not see a motive for her to do so—but he could not muster any anger. He felt empty and numb. His thoughts were unable to coalesce into anything coherent.

All that morning the cook had been restless. She kept going back and forth across the kitchen and could not sit still. She waited for the other servants to start shouting about the monster prince's magical metamorphosis into a dashing, ravishing fully human prince. She found it hard to breathe. Her shaking hands kept missing the vegetables she was supposed to be cutting, and her fingers bled lightly in various places where the poorly aimed knife had fallen.

But she heard nothing about the expected great magical transformation. Instead, she heard just the usual everyday back and forth banter about this errand and that laundry and the rude dressmaker coming late for the queen's fitting. Still, the monster had not shown himself for breakfast. So the cook was not sure what to think. Perhaps he was planning a grand entrance to show off his new handsome human head.

Her curiosity finally got the better of her. She had to see what had happened—she could not take the waiting any longer. So the cook mixed a salad of leaves and grass, spiced with olive oil and garlic, placed it into a great bowl, and went to the monster's bedroom.

She knocked gently at the closed door.

No answer.

She knocked again.

Still no answer.

The cook pushed the door open. There was still not a sound. She walked in, and there she saw the monster, and he was still every bit a monster. He was perfectly still and his eyes seemed dulled and focused on a distant point far behind the wall at which he was staring. The cook put the bowl down on the Minotaur's desk and closed the door. She sat on a stool next to the monster's desk facing him, although she averted her eyes, which were drawn involuntarily to the floor.

Did you try the potion?

Yes. The voice was whispered and hollow.

Did you follow the red witch's instructions?

Yes, each and every one.

Well, don't despair. Spells can be tricky you know. They can take time to get right. Maybe an ingredient was mixed up. I will send word to the witch, discreetly, and we will get you something that will work.

The cook stood up. She straightened her dress and apron. She walked out of the monster's room, quietly and swiftly; her eyes never left the floor.

The monster looked up at her as she walked away. He reflected that she was a kindly soul. Her words had cheered him somewhat. Perhaps she was right—the witch only needed some time to tinker and fine tune her work. What was he so distraught about? The Minotaur wondered. He only needed the spell to work once. If it took a dozen tries, so be it. Once the magic did its work properly, he would be freed forever from the curse of being a monster and could live the rest of his life as a happy man.

The monster let out a sigh and slapped his knees. He got up, grabbed the bowl of salad, and devoured it eagerly. He was going to wait and be a good and respectful patient—if that was the right word. He would ask the Red Princess to try her sorcery again. He chose to trust her and to commit himself to her care. Over and over again, the monster told himself, the spell only needed to work once, just once, and everything would be fixed. A hundred failures made no difference so long as there was, at last, the one crowning ultimate success.

The Minotaur was not kept in suspense long. The Red Princess had been as anxious as the monster and the cook, and had sent a young servant—in reality a witch's apprentice—to the cook that morning. Upon learning the potion had had no effect, the Red Princess became concerned. She did not want the queen to believe she had failed her son, the monster prince. That could unravel her carefully laid schemes to establish a presence at court. And also, she continued to herself, who knew what the monster would do? He was docile and tame that night, when he was hopeful. But disappointment had led more than one witch's client to fury and violence— and those were customers who were not part bull, and had no horns for goring a poor witch. This situation required careful handling.

The Red Princess sent her apprentice back to the cook with two items: a small bottle and a written message. The Red Princess had thought of conveying her message in person, but reflected that she did not want to be in the same room as a bull bitter from disappointment. Wounded beasts, she thought, often lash out.

The Red Princess explained to her apprentice, who explained to the cook, who whispered it to the monster at a secret nighttime rendezvous near the kitchen pantry: Drink this bottle tonight and go to sleep. If the transformation has not taken effect by morning, read and follow the message in the scroll. The Red Princess and her apprentice each delivered the message in a flat, even tone. But the cook could not contain her hope and excitement and her voice, even in a whisper, rose slightly and her words toppled rapidly one on top of each other.

The monster felt relieved at the witch's newly supplied revised remedy. He took the bottle and scroll firmly in his hand, thanked the cook sincerely for her kindness and discretion, and walked vigorously back to his bed chamber. He pulled the stopper out of the little glass bottle and sniffed the light blue liquid. It smelled of flowers, which the monster took as a good omen—flowers reminded him of his midnight talks with Ariadne in the palace gardens. He took a deep breath and raised the bottle to his lips. He hesitated at first, but then poured the bottle's contents quickly down his throat. The monster swallowed so quickly, in fact, that he let out a belch loud enough he feared waking his mother. He had barely tasted the liquid, but it was thin and watery, and washed down easily. There was no uncomfortable lingering aftertaste this time.

The draught did not make the monster drowsy. The monster laboriously arranged his blankets, more to take his mind off the magic than to accomplish any actual purpose in enhancing his sleep. He lay down on his side and stared at the fig tree branches poking through the window and into his room. He thought, for a fleeting moment, of climbing down into the garden, searching for Ariadne, and telling her he would soon be fully human, indeed, the most handsome human boy in all of Crete and a royal prince to boot. Still, he was afraid that she would laugh at him again. Better to wait until the spell actually succeeded, the Minotaur reflected, and then Ariadne would hear how handsome he had become and she would beg for a chance to stroll with him in the gardens. That stroll would make all her scheming friends seethe with envy. Maybe the monster, once he was no longer a monster, would make her wait a little while for the privilege of a private discussion with the beautiful prince—not too long, but just a little, to wash out that laughter from her soul. Those sweet visions rocked the monster to sleep.

Yet the next morning proved to be another cruel disappointment. The Minotaur sat up and yawned when he woke. As he lowered his hands from stretching for the long yawn he felt his horns again. Once more, the spell had failed.

A wave of numb despair passed through his body, but the monster told himself to be brave and to persevere. He must not give up. The witch had planned for this possibility and had sent a note with some kind of contingency instructions. Right, the Minotaur thought, time to read the note and follow the next set of directions:

Dearest Prince,

If the medicines I have brewed and supplied have not worked, then you must go to the shrine of the great goddess, Aphrodite. It lies to the west of Knossos on the slopes of Mount Psiloritis, birthplace of the mighty Zeus. There is a grove there sacred to Aphrodite where she helps the ugly and cursed become young and beautiful, so they may end their heartaches. Follow the main road leading west from the city gate, and take it to the high mountain. The goddess will have mercy upon you and your sufferings.

Your ever loyal and humble servant ....

V. The Monster's Journey to the Shrine of the Goddess

THE MONSTER READ the short note many times, although he could not figure out why he did so; the words did not change as he reread them. The note left him torn: While the witch had clearly given up on his cause and abandoned him, she did present an alternate path to redemption—should he be bold enough to take it. The monster had never traveled outside of the palace complex or, to be more precise, the queen's tower and the palace gardens. He had lived his life in gilded confinement, but now he was being told to leave.

The prospect of a journey beyond the palace was both terrifying and exciting. He had often dreamed of adventures beyond the palace and in his mind had journeyed through rough seas and foreign battlefields. But he had never mustered the courage to try to leave his familiar grounds. Traveling away was always, in the monster's mind, something for the future, when he would perform great deeds or maybe marry Ariadne or, in his truly ambitious fantasies, both. The time for such wandering and leaving was never in the now; it was always going to happen at some unspecified later time. So the monster was able, in his dreams, to feel both wholly confident in his appetite for adventure and his utter lack of need to act upon that confidence in any immediately foreseeable future.

In fact, the Minotaur was scared of how lonely he would be without his mother's warm affection, and he was worried about his safety in the outside world, as he thought of it. There was no way to know whether some overeager hunter would try to poach him, judging the monster to be in the category of beasts instead of the category of people. The Minotaur had read enough tales of monster-slaying derring-do by fearless heroes to be leery of being a monster tourist on his own on a country road.

On the other hand, the monster reflected, what choice did he have? Trapped in his cursed monster body, the Minotaur could not marry the girl whom he loved, or any other girl for that matter. His mother was kind, but she would grow old and die—and who would shelter the palace's monster then? The monster simply had no logical role in palace life other than that of a monster, and the only role assigned to a monster was to terrify and punish, usually in a suitably violent mode, and then be heroically slaughtered in vengeance for his atrocious crimes. The Minotaur, however, did not want to commit any crimes and certainly dreaded the thought of the hero's hand of death reaching for him with a sharp swinging weapon. Since meeting Ariadne, his dreams had been banal and sentimental to an absurd degree: The monster dreamt only of marriage, holding hands with his beloved, walking through fields, and hugging their lovely brood of small children. He had no appetite for savagery and fighting. Still, he knew there were no singing monsters in Crete's fields and vineyards. The Minotaur knew there was simply no way to persuade the people of Crete to include a monster in their everyday dullness. Monsters were meant for extremes—violent extremes—and not the small pleasures of the homebody. The Minotaur could not live the life that he wanted, in his estimation, without changing his fate. He knew he must end his monsterhood once and for all.

And if that meant a daring escape from the palace and a pilgrimage to the shrine of the great goddess Aphrodite, then so be it, thought the monster. He took a deep breath and closed his eyes. He calmed his raging nerves by force of his will. His course was decided: He would escape—the palace, his curse, his fate as a monster. The monster would change his life, permanently.

The Minotaur began his preparations. He waited for a time when the cook was out. He snuck into the kitchen where he filled a bag with grass and a small, lightweight earthenware bottle with watered down wine—provisions for the journey. He decided to depart that night after the queen and her household had fallen asleep. He found it difficult to make conversation with his mother over dinner. He wanted to tell her of his plans, but was afraid that she—or one of her servants—would try to stop him. One word to the guards would be enough; the monster could not take the chance. So with his head swirling with fantasies of happy transformations and terrifying fear of the unknown out there beyond the palace, the Minotaur willed himself to be interested in Queen Pasiphae's plans to improve the quality of her bed sheets (which she swore gave her a terrible rash). He forced upon himself an interest in her sleep troubles and even mustered a suggestion about what fabric textures induced rest and healthy skin.

The monster knew he was deceiving his mother and she would be hurt and worried when he disappeared suddenly. But then, he thought, he had no choice. His mother had been unable—or perhaps less charitably, unwilling—to fight for the Minotaur to have some productive role in court life. More galling, he thought, she had done nothing herself to lift his curse. It occurred to him she could have, but did not, consult with witches or go begging the goddess at her sacred shrine. No, Queen Pasiphae smothered her monster boy with warmth, but had passively accepted his cursed fate. The Minotaur was filled with loathing at his mother's failure to fight for him. He felt alone in his struggle.

Perhaps it was worse than that, he thought. Maybe his mother preferred him to remain a monster. As a monster he was trapped in her tower. He could not grow up and do what men did—marry, fight, manage an estate, have children, serve in the government. He was unable to leave his childhood world because there was nowhere else for him to go. His mother wanted this never-ending childhood, the monster thought bitterly: her vulnerable little boy who could never grow up and leave her. The monster was her doll, and she had made sure he could never leave her carefully furnished, dainty, pretty dollhouse in the corner of the palace grounds.

Now the Minotaur had worked himself into a fit of righteous indignation. Underneath that sweet surface his mother had wronged him and treated him unjustly. She had colluded in his curse and his fate, and she wanted him penned in forever to be her plaything. The monster decided he had had enough. He would grow up and leave. He would go to the shrine of the goddess and secure divine dispensation to be made human, completely human. His mother would have no ability to stop him, as a fully human prince, from growing up and doing the deeds of a grown man.

That night the monster lay awake and alert in his bedchamber. He could not have fallen asleep even if he had tried (which he did not). The Minotaur listened closely to the sounds from his mother's bedchamber: banter with the servant, which sounded so loud that night, chests opening and closing, bottles popping open, and all sorts of creaks and squeaks against the floor. He grew angrier as he listened closely, reflecting in his bitterness that none of these nattering hens cared about his lack of a future or his inability to move on to some normal, real, productive life. His blood pumped harder, fueled by surging waves of self-pity. It seemed to the Minotaur those women would never stop their yelling and creaking and door banging, and just calm down and get to sleep.

Nonetheless, eventually, as always, the lights faded and the various choking, gasping snores filled the air, a chorus of uncoordinated, off-key growling and screeching. The monster clenched his fists and knitted his brow. Now was the time; yes now, no more delay. He had to act. He quickly donned a thick winter cloak made of cheap, thick brown fabric. It had a wide hood, which would conceal his monstrous bull's head as he traveled. He crept stealthily out of his room and up to the fifth floor of the tower. The monster still recalled the secret tunnel to the stables, although he had not used it for many years.

He groped clumsily through the dark junkyard on the fifth floor, banging and bumping into various objects. The monster was scared that these noises would stir the queen or her servants out of bed, but they did not. Eventually reaching the back, he easily pulled the rusted lock off the door of the secret walkway.

The monster walked through the tunnel in the dark, trying to be as quiet as he could. It was a tighter fit than the Minotaur remembered (although those were the memories of his young boyhood, when the bull's head was still a calf's head) and he was bent over the whole way. Midway through the tunnel his feet froze, and his body felt pinned down by regret. Perhaps this was a bad idea; his mother did love him, and her choice to coddle him in her tower may have been a wise decision. It was her way to keep him safe. Perhaps he was veering headlong into the crosshairs of a

bloodthirsty hunter and would-be hero who would fell him with a swift series of arrows. This could easily happen if he was caught unawares sleeping
in the woods.

The monster almost persuaded himself to turn back, but then he saw
Ariadne again in his mind, with her petite swaying body and cascading long
brown hair, and she was still cruelly mocking him with her laughter. The
monster's disappointed love could only be a farce so long as he was trapped
in his hideous, disgusting body. He thought Ariadne was right to scorn him;
monsters were not fit lovers and bridegrooms. The Minotaur agreed with
her; it was ridiculous to imagine a fierce, terrible monster as a swooning,
aching would-be lover. He had to change his fate. He walked forward again.

The monster exited the tunnel into the royal stables. Everyone was
asleep. He found a horse in a corner, already saddled. He mounted it and
tugged at the reins. The monster had read many poems about horseback
riding, but had never actually ridden one. He was scared, but he needed to
get away from the palace by some means or other. Luckily for the monster,
the horse was tame and obliging. The Minotaur trotted out of the stables
towards a gate. There was a sentry posted to the side of the gate. The monster said nothing, but motioned with his hand to open the gate. The sentry
on duty obeyed. The monster reasoned that the sentry must have thought
the hooded rider was a secret messenger of the king on the type of midnight assignment where questions were not asked.

The horse briskly strode forward beyond the palace gates and onto a
road. The monster looked about until he saw a large mountain rising to the
west, and then he rode towards it. By dawn, the monster had cleared the
city boundaries and was riding on a road through the countryside, abutted
by forest on its sides.

The monster's worries returned. He would be easier to spot in the
daylight. Questions would no doubt be asked about the stolen horse. So he
stopped, dismounted, tied the horse to a nearby tree, and walked into a
nearby wood. The monster strode quickly through the dense cluster of trees
until he reached a huge, towering, gnarled old tree. The Minotaur climbed
the tree, up to its top branches. He was hidden from sight by the thick
foliage and his new hideout had the added benefit of a wonderful breakfast
of fresh leaves.

The monster ate and rested his tired limbs on the thick, high branch. He felt marvelously free, floating. For the first time the monster had no constraints to burden him. As long as he was not caught, the Minotaur could do anything he wanted to, whenever he wanted to—no tower, no mother, no guards, just himself and the branches and the breeze from the sea. He loved the feel of the air on his body; he had not noticed before how musty and stale the air had grown in his bedchamber. The monster felt the sky had never been so gloriously blue before. Everything was possible, and the glorious future happiness of which he dreamed would soon be at hand once he reached the great goddess Aphrodite and secured her blessing to remove his undeserved curse.

The monster traveled the highway to the western mountain by night and slept and rested in the high tree branches by day. He would amble down his chosen tree towards dusk and begin his nocturnal walk. The trees grew denser as he walked away from Knossos and towards the mountain. The brown branches and green foliage soon blocked the setting sun, which only sprinkled down to the path in scattered pink dots. The forest seemed to be reaching down to suffocate its apparently unwelcome guests on the road. In this, the forest was helped by the stifling late summer humid heat, which made the air heavy and hard to breathe, and bathed the monster in his sweat.

There was something hostile and forbidding about the forest. There were no flowers or fruits; only black dirt, brown branches, green leaves, and dirty little rocks, which were good for absent-minded kicking. Every once in a while the monster would hear some small animal or bird flee up a tree or under a bush. He never saw them, but he could clearly hear the desperate, panicked speed of their little legs and wings. They were all hiding from something or fleeing from something. Perhaps they too were scared of the forest suffocating them.

One such lonely twilight the Minotaur passed an abandoned shrine. It was nestled in a small clearing just off the side of the road. A circular stone floor had been laid down on the ground, although weeds were popping up in the cracks in the fraying stone. On one side of this floor was a circular wall, which depicted a hunting scene in a carved relief. The stone had faded so that it was hard for the monster to make out exactly what was depicted.

It seemed that a man was poised to hurl a javelin at a beast of some kind; the beast did not run away, but was charging at him with tusks or horns or some type of fearsome appendage. The monster could not tell which side would prevail, the noble man or the monstrous beast; although he somehow felt the whole confrontation was all a great unnecessary mistake. There was no need for these two to try to kill each other, in his mind. The monster further wondered what kind of malevolent deity would glory in this type of ugly battle.

Opposite the relief was a statue. The statue was broken. It had no head or arms, but still had a torso and both legs. From their position it seemed that whoever was depicted in the statue was running towards the altar, but was frozen in stone for some reason by some god, as if in punishment for a transgression. Perhaps, the monster thought, the intruder was rushing to break up the fight between man and beast, and the angry god of the forest shrine turned him to stone. It was as if the forest had murdered and frozen whatever tentative foothold human kindness had made.

The relief proved to be prophetic, after a fashion. The next day, in the early afternoon, the monster was resting in a tree, high up on a firm branch, when he heard angry cries—men's angry cries, followed by wildly barking dogs. The Minotaur was terrified—could these men be hunting him? Had he been found before he could reach the shrine of the goddess? He tightened his grip and slowly shifted position so he could see the ground better. There were two young men running with a pack of dogs. The two men were both sporting daggers on their belts. Their movements were quick and assured. The monster caught sight of one of the pairs of eyes, which flashed a grim, humorless determination to do some task at hand.

The young men and their dogs ran right past the monster's tree and further into the forest. His grip on the branch relaxed slightly, but he continued to watch the two young men closely. He looked ahead, slightly in front of them, and saw a large deer, with a speckled orange hide and high antlers, jumping up over a rock to escape the dogs. But the dear stumbled in his landing and fell, and one of the dogs flew, jaw first, into the deer's rear left leg and tore viciously at the deer's flesh with sharp, glinting teeth. The wound bled rapidly and the stumbling deer slipped and fell in its own blood when it tried to stand up again. Now the dogs piled upon the wounded animal, tearing at various parts of his body as he thrashed and flailed helplessly.

The two young men walked over to the deer's head. They crouched down, grinning broadly. One of them laughed and chided the tortured animal for giving them such a difficult chase. The other man commented that the dogs would have full bellies soon. The laughing man grabbed one set of antlers in his hand, cut it loose with his long dagger, and then made short work of the other set of antlers. The deer's eyes looked up in agony and disbelief. One of the men yawned and, appearing bored with the whole exercise, cut the deer's throat so that he could move on with his day. The dying body rattled pitifully. The two men paid it no attention.

The monster watched the two handsome young men as they went away with satisfied grins and lazy steps. He looked at the deer's corpse for a long time. The monster reflected on the dividing line between a man and a beast: Men can see each other's pain, but not their prey's. Beasts were for killing and taunting. The monster felt the gods had shown him this scene as a warning. The monster kept his silent vigil over the abandoned corpse until dusk, when he climbed down the tree and dug a grave for the deer. He wondered whether the ferryman demanded payment from the shades of animals also to cross the River Styx. The monster was not sure, so, to be safe, he placed two coins over the deer's eyes and then laid the beast to rest in a hastily dug, shallow grave.

Loneliness started to gnaw at the traveling monster. All his life he had been fussed over by his mother and a parade of nosy servants. He had never felt completely alone, even when he was by himself in his bed-chamber, as the attending throng was only a slender wall away. At first, his newfound forest solitude was exhilarating: no one to watch him or con-strain him or take him to task.

Yet the monster soon missed the company of others. He now felt trapped inside his own mind. He grew bored rehashing the same thoughts to himself again and again. He was starved for mental stimulation.

One such lonely, brooding afternoon the monster stared blankly down at the road from his perch on a high branch. The hot mid-afternoon sun burned his human skin and bull's hide, and he could not find a comfortable position no matter which way he turned or shimmied. The monster hoped something on the road would distract him.

This hope was often in vain. There were few travelers on the road. The monster sometimes wondered whether he was headed in the right direction, but then he would notice the high mountain peak in the west; so perhaps the loneliness of the road was owed to the unpopularity of Aphrodite's shrine. Maybe gods went through waves of rising and declining popularity, the monster thought. Or maybe this was the shrine's off-season, as the harvest was not yet complete. Would-be pilgrims had to finish their labors in the fields first.

This uncomfortable, sweaty afternoon proved to be different. The monster saw a young girl walking on the road. She was quite young, probably even slightly younger than Ariadne. Her body appeared only to have recently started to develop the features of a maturing woman. Despite the scorching heat and thick humidity, she wore an elaborate black headdress, which included an opaque black veil. She was crying behind this veil, in loud but muffled sobs, which echoed in the surrounding woods. Her steps were slow and labored. She seemed to follow her companion as if she lacked any will of her own. This companion held the girl by the hand and, walking in front of her, pulled her along. The girl seemed almost devoid of any desire to move at all, although her companion seemed determined to march down the road in the direction towards the goddess Aphrodite's shrine.

This lone companion was an older man. He was tall, lean, and narrow in his shoulders. His hair was sparse but still dark. He had a mangy beard, which had recently gone to seed from lack of proper care. This man often looked down at the ground. He never attempted to lift or remove the veil, even though the monster thought it must be difficult to have one's only traveling companion be a crying, faceless black ghost who must be sweating terribly. The man constantly sighed and shook his head. He occasionally squeezed and kissed the girl's hand and whispered some inaudible message to her.

As this strange pair was heading in the same direction—they by day and he by night—the monster, somewhat naturally, found himself to be following them. Whatever conversation they had was impossible to hear from the tree tops, but the monster could tell they seemed to speak to each other every now and then. Both ate sparingly, just small nibbles on bread and cheese they had brought along in a sack. The monster wondered how they had the strength to walk the forest road, with its rocks on the ground and winding ascents, on such empty bellies.

The monster's loneliness finally got the better of him. These two were apparently his only opportunity for company, he thought, so he would try to speak to them. If nothing else, maybe he could learn the mystery of the girl's strange, uncomfortable veiling.

One late afternoon the Minotaur saw the pair walking on the road by his tree. He waited for them to reach a point a bit ahead of his perch, and then he quietly climbed down his tree. The monster slouched and pulled the hood over his head, so his face would not be visible at a distance. Once his clothes were suitably adjusted, he walked forward in the direction of the veiled girl and her companion.

The monster's long legs, with their wide strides, quickly caught up with the languid girl and her companion. When the Minotaur was slightly behind them, he called out a greeting. The two stopped walking and swiveled around to face the tall, hulking hooded figure. The man reached for a dagger and demanded to know if the monster was a bandit. If so, the bandit should know there was nothing to steal, but the man had been a veteran of more than one foreign battle campaign and could still hold his ground in a fight.

I am no bandit, the monster replied. I am a pilgrim, to the shrine of the great goddess Aphrodite. I have been cursed by an evil witch's spell, which is why I must hide my face on this journey. If you were to see my face you would run in terror. But I am not a monster, no matter how I may a look. I am a man who has been wronged, and I hope to beg the goddess's blessing to remove my affliction. The road is lonely, and I was hoping maybe for some friendly company. And if you do meet real bandits, or wolves, I will be a useful second hand in defense of the young lady.

The man relaxed his grip on his dagger, although he did not put it back in its sheath. His eyes looked straight at the monster's hood. The girl moved behind the man, so that he was in between her and the monster.

What exactly is this affliction? What happened to you?

As I said, I was cursed by a witch. I was a guard in the service of King Minos, and I policed the safety of Knossos. I was betrothed to a lovely girl, a merchant's daughter, in fact. I had met her after I chased a gang of robbers away from her father's store. The old man had promised to take me into his business once we married. The future was looking good for me.

Until one night my commander ordered me to a tavern. There was a great brawl going: chairs flying, wine barrels overturned, the tavern waitresses ducking under tables in the corner. After I separated what seemed to be the two sides and smacked the ringleaders around a bit, for their own good if you ask me, I found out the whole thing had started because one man accused the other man's wife of using witchcraft to drug him to sleep so that his wife could visit her young lover. The alleged witch's husband denied his wife was anything but a sweet, tame homebody. After getting everyone off to bed and helping straighten up the tavern a bit (the owner was a good friend to us guards, always good for a free drink), I decided to investigate this supposed witch the next day. If she was doing something to disturb the public peace of Knossos, then we had to get her in line.

I went to her house the next morning. Her husband was out, at his job—a blacksmith, as a matter of fact, a good one too. I guess his bruises healed fast. Or he preferred not being alone too much with his wife. Anyway, I arrived at the house, knocked, and she was alone. She invited me in and offered me some wine. I told her about the fight from the previous night and that I was following up the accusations leveled against her person, standard procedure and such. No, she assured me, this was all untrue. Everyone in the neighborhood knew that the man's wife was cheating on her husband with a porter who lived in a basement room across the courtyard, and it had nothing to do with her. She said the whole thing came from the fact that the wronged husband became drunk and wanted to pick a fight with someone from the courtyard. He saw her husband, and the fight was on, his ridiculous pretext being that she was a witch.

Stupid me, I believed every word of these lies. Soon enough, though, this woman—this witch—crossed my path everywhere. She bumped into me when I made my rounds through Knossos. She was there at the tavern. When I left the barracks at night to relieve myself, there she was again, watching me.

All this creeping and following made me uncomfortable. So I paid her another visit. Once more, there was no husband at home. I asked her why she was following me. What, she said, don't you like having me around? She slipped out of her robe and stood there naked. We could be great friends, she said. My husband will not return for hours, and my soft sheets are on my bed in the room just over there. Let me tell you, it was tempting. She was a gorgeous woman, tall like a statue and with an amazing head of thick, long red hair. Still, I was engaged, and I was not about to cheat on my fiancé. So I told her, put on your robe and let's keep clear of each other. Your husband is an honest man and he deserves better. She said fine, put her robe on, and smiled at me. You're right, she said, I have been acting like a silly little girl. Oh wait, she added, I promised my husband I would give you a little bottle of wine in gratitude for helping him home the other night. Please wait here, it will not take me long to find the bottle I had picked out.

Then she disappeared into the back. I heard her rummaging through something. I decided to stay because I thought it would be rude to leave and to refuse her gift. And maybe the wine would turn out to be pretty good. She finally came out, gave me the bottle, and said goodbye. Alright, I thought to myself, that problem has been solved, and it was time to move on.

What a fool I turned out to be. That evening I opened the bottle in the barracks and took a drink. I was exhausted from the long day, so instead of drinking the whole bottle I took a nap. When I woke up my head had turned into a bull's head. That wine was cursed. It was a spell to turn me into a bull. I was only saved because I had just drunk a little bit, so only my head was transformed. Still, I cannot go around with a bull's head, and my wedding is off if I cannot fix this curse. My future father-in-law was very clear that my scary new head would not be good for his store's business. So I talked to my fiancé and her father, and we decided that I would make a pilgrimage to the great goddess Aphrodite's shrine in the western mountain. That is where I was heading when I met you two on this road.

The man put his dagger back in its sheath. He smiled broadly at the story.

Teach you to poke around other people's business too much.

I know. I cannot wait to leave the guards, become a merchant—fabrics and dyes, by the way, if you ever need any—and stick to my own problems. Raise a pack of little ones to help in the store.

Can you pull your hood down? I want to see the witch's handiwork, if you don't mind. Make sure you are being honest with me. I cannot be too careful on these roads, especially with my young daughter.

The monster stepped forward, and pulled his hood down to his shoulders. His bull's head and horns were now revealed. The man flinched and gaped. The veiled girl circled from behind her father and tilted her head slightly in the direction of the monstrous and terrifying head.

You really were telling the truth. You look practically like that flesh-eating monster that King Minos keeps locked up somewhere in the palace.

The Minotaur bit his tongue. He forced himself to appear relaxed.

Still, we could use the extra muscle. A palace guardsman could be helpful here. I do not trust the quiet of this place. There is something foul here waiting to pounce upon us. I feel in my bones that somewhere nearby there must be robbers who drove all the foot traffic away from this road. Probably sitting high up in the tree branches and waiting for the right moment. They'll think twice when they see you.

The man laughed expansively, and his laugh echoed against the silence of the forest. The echo bounced back and around, each time more hollow and ghostly until it lost all human aspect. The monster smiled and shook the man's hand; he had, by dint of his ingenuity, become a fellow man and temporarily shed his role as a monster. The girl said nothing.

The three walked on together. The monster pulled his hood up again, so as not to frighten (as he explained to the man) any passersby they might encounter. The man agreed this was a wise precaution. The two men walked ahead while the girl stumbled clumsily a few paces behind them. As the two men talked, their walking pace accelerated unconsciously, and they repeatedly had to stop or slow themselves to avoid losing the slow-moving girl in the rear.

The monster asked the man about where he had come from, why they were traveling this road, and why the young girl wore a thick black veil in the burning, humid sun. The man explained that he was a landowner in the countryside not far from Knossos. He grew grapes and pressed them into wine. He was sure that the guardsmen had all tasted his excellent products in the Knossos taverns. Some of his wines were even shipped to the Greek mainland and beyond, some even as far as the cities of Sicily.

While he had fought bravely, if not recklessly, in Crete's foreign wars as a young man and rose to become an officer, he had suffered a horrible fall from a horse during a training exercise in Knossos. His leg took months to heal. The king, on the recommendation of the regiment's physician, granted a medical discharge and a modest pension. The man moved to the countryside where his older sister and her husband lived. He helped out on their farm as best he could, but the move was tough: The man had been born and reared in Knossos, in the loud crashing crowds of the great metropolis, and the farm's quiet and solitude unnerved him at first. Still, he resigned himself to his fate and learned to adjust. After a while he even enjoyed the country life. He learned to look forward to sunrises and sunsets and to the taste of fresh milk and cheese.

There was a neighboring landowner with a wine press. This gentleman was a widower with an only daughter, an unexpected child of his old age. The man was old and sick, and he worried about his daughter's future. He took a liking to the military veteran and thought that both his fighting skills and guaranteed pension payments could help safeguard the estate and his girl. The match was made, and the man moved from his sister's house to his father-in-law's house, and he learned the art of growing grapes and making wine. Two years into the marriage the old estate owner died, and the man became a country squire.

The man seemed to be blessed by the gods. The estate thrived and expanded, and he was able to acquire some adjacent lots. He became an official in the local village government and worked with his neighbors to drive a pack of bandits out of the area. He meted out justice fairly and was so well-regarded that landowners from far away would ask his assistance in mediating their disputes.

The greatest blessing was the children: five in all, tall strapping girls. Some of his friends grumbled that the man was being punished for his arrogant good fortune by being denied a son, but the man thought this was nonsense. He loved being a father to girls. Sons, he thought, remembering his own boyhood, butted up against their fathers and struggled for supremacy.

Boys did not listen and had to be brought to heel with hard discipline, like hung over infantrymen who needed a whipping from their officers. Fathering a son was a grinding burden.

Girls, however, were altogether different. While they scratched like vicious cats with their mothers (and could mothers and daughters ever fight—and about what he never could understand), with their father his girls were playful, kind, sweet, and affectionate. They liked to sit on his lap on long rainy afternoons and listen to his memories of old wars or tales of squabbles in the countryside. They listened closely to his lectures on grape-growing and wine-pressing. Sometimes when he saw one of his girls playing around in the courtyard in front of the villa he would sneak over, pick her up, and kiss her cheeks all over. The girl would squeal with delight.

His favorite daughter was the eldest. She had a sharp mind, smarter than most men, he felt, and he would secretly consult with her when he had to decide a difficult case between feuding landowners. Although she lacked experience in life, she could, when she chose, unleash a ferocious torrent of logic upon any problem. Her father was dazzled when his eldest girl applied her mental faculties to the fullest. He imagined that someday she would reign supreme as the grand lady of an estate. He tried not to think about what her husband would be like: He did not want a weak vacillating man, but he felt that a proud man would feel the need to belittle his girl's superb intelligence to show he was master of his household.

The girl, unfortunately, had reached the same conclusion. Her body blossomed and matured. She lost interest in her father. What she wanted now was the attention of the local boys. She learned quickly that handsome boys were not interested in her opinions, much less the slicing logic she could apply to their foolish and insecure boasts. So she became a flirt and learned that volleys of teases and slight brushes of skin could get her the attention she craved. These changes depressed her father, but what could he do? Her mother assured him that all girls go through these silly phases, but she would grow out of it.

The girl's heart settled on one boy, a son of a prosperous farmer. Fortunately, the farmer's boy loved her in return. The man thought the young man was not a bad sort, and the boy even let his daughter express her opinions without trying to hush her or show some feigned superiority. Everything seemed in place for a happy wedding.

Except, though, there was one other boy who took the girl's flirty teases in a far too serious vein. This boy was the son of the local cobbler and apparently was a highly strung, too serious young man. He worked day and night learning the cobbler's craft with a fanatical perfectionism; any shoe that fit less than perfectly drove him into a furious, stampeding rage. He would rework shoes until he had realized his vision. There were many complaints about the excessive time it took to acquire a new pair of shoes or to mend old ones, but as there were no other cobblers nearby, the residents of the area had no choice but to make due with the frequent delays and occasional screaming outbursts of the talented but forbidding cobbler's apprentice.

The cobbler's apprentice had been forced one day by his more sensible father to take a rest. The apprentice walked off to a nearby lake determined to have the perfect rest by the water with a fishing rod. He sat, scowling, concentrating hard on the act of resting. But he kept feeling ever more tense and angry because he could not master the art of relaxation. Unfortunately for her, the girl happened by the lake and saw the odd sight of a young boy about her age holding a fishing rod like a sword and looking at the lake with eyes of focused, driven hate. The contrast between the boy's absurd earnestness and the frivolousness of his actual task made the girl peel over with merry, singsong laughter. The cobbler's apprentice was flustered at first and turned menacingly in the direction of the mocking laughter, but his face froze and flushed red when he saw her—she was certainly pretty, too much so for her own good. She walked to him and tousled his hair and teased him about being overly serious; she told him he would be handsome if he could only stop frowning. And then she added more coquettish remarks in this vein. The cobbler's apprentice could only muster a meager parade of halting one word responses: yes; no; maybe; perhaps; sure; alright; and so on and so forth. The girl eventually went on her way, thinking little of this harmless adventure.

But the cobbler's apprentice now burned with love as seriously as he had burned with the drive to make perfect shoes. He became distracted in his work and made careless errors as he could think of nothing but the girl he now loved. He decided he must wed her. He planned his arguments for asking her father for her hand: his skill as a cobbler, the family's shoe-making and repairing monopoly in the area, a willingness to accept minimal, even no dowry—no small favor to a father stuck with marrying off five girls. The more the young man mulled the matter over in his mind, the clearer his case became to him. It seemed to the cobbler's apprentice that he was the girl's one true, proper suitor. Soon he had convinced himself she belonged to him as of right, like the cobbler's shop he was set to inherit.

So one could only imagine the shock to the young man when the an-nouncement was made that the girl was betrothed to the farmer's son. He refused to believe the news when he first heard it, and was only convinced of the truth when he tried to approach the girl's father, who politely, but gently, told him his daughter had already chosen her future husband.

The father's words made the cobbler's apprentice fume. He had so convinced himself of his right to possess the girl that her choice of another struck him as a betrayal, if not adultery. In his fevered brain, he had con-vinced himself he had been terribly wronged by the woman who should be his wife. He decided he must be avenged. By some means or other he came into possession of a small bottle of a clear liquid, a liquid that appeared to be water, but was not.

The cobbler's apprentice followed the girl around at night, hounding her around corners, waiting for a moment when she was alone. The girl still did not take him seriously and would stick out her tongue and laugh when she saw him. He was a silly fool, lurking in the blurred background edges of her life. She would soon learn how mistaken this smug, superior perspective was. It was the way of monsters to lurk at the edges of life, before they lashed out and changed everything.

One clear evening the girl walked alone on a small bridge, leaned her arms over the railing's edge, and dreamed her happy dreams of her be-trothed and their future life together. The cobbler's apprentice saw his chance. He walked briskly up to her. She turned and faced him, looking puzzled. What could he want? But then he pulled the bottle from his pocket, removed the stopper, and splashed the girl's face with the liquid that looked like water, but was not water. He stepped back and waited. He watched, grinning madly.

The girl screamed in pain—her face burned terribly; it was on fire from the liquid. She could not see, she screamed for help, for real water to wash off the trick burning water. Now, though, the cobbler's apprentice laughed and told his tale to her writhing, grasping body—of his right to her hand in matrimony, of her betrayal of him, and of his revenge. He walked away with even strides, quite satisfied, and left her wailing in pain.

By some means or other the girl made it home that night. Her face was horribly scarred. The burning water had twisted and burned and shriveled much of the skin on her face. She was no longer young and beautiful. When he saw her ruined, charred face, her beloved, the farmer's son, renounced the engagement. He was beautiful and deemed himself thereby entitled to a wife who was equally beautiful. He knew his action was cruel, but he told himself the gods had cursed the girl, clearly, with her deformity, and the gods are just, so she must have committed some horrible wicked deeds in secret. Indeed, the farmer's son went so far as to offer thanks to the gods for exposing the girl's true nature before he married her and she bore his children.

The girl's mother wrote her off: No one would marry the monstrous hag, and there were four other sisters who needed husbands, so she urged her husband to send the disgusting creature off somewhere to beg for alms. The mother could not bear the sight of her. Egged on by their mother, the girl's sisters—who had always been jealous of her pretty face, their father's favor, and the easy way she had always had of sucking up all of the boys' attentions—piled on with their insults, telling her that an ugly, deformed girl could have no husband and no future. One especially spiteful sister offered to employ her as a maid, so long as she would keep her ogre face buried in the laundry and the cooking pots. The mother and sisters told themselves they were not being cruel, but simply facing up to hard realities and doing the crippled girl the favor of being honest with her and not letting her linger in false hope.

The girl was reeling: from beauty to beast, in one dizzying instant. She felt hopeless and saw no future for herself. She did not want to live the life of an ugly monstrous girl, and she could not bear being ignored or shunned. She thought about suicide, and even considered jumping from that same small bridge, although she worried that the drop was too small to do much injury.

But her father had given her hope again. He alone had never given up on her, and he defended his eldest daughter when her mother and sisters were cruel to her. He loved his eldest daughter tenderly, from the time that she, only two years old, had crawled onto his lap one night and stroked his cheek and tried to feed him some nuts. He could not bear the thought of a world without this daughter. He knew that she needed hope, though, to go on, and so her father promised to take her to the shrine of the great goddess Aphrodite on the sacred mountain. Aphrodite will see your goodness and your wisdom, he said, and restore your outer beauty to be again the match of your inner beauty. Pray to the goddess and she will heal you.

The father commissioned the nearest tailor to make an elaborate headdress with a thick black veil, so that his daughter could walk on the road without displaying her shame. The father had led his veiled daughter by the hand along the long road that would lead to the grove of the goddess on the mountain. He had guided her slow movements as she could not see easily through the black veil. He had assured her again and again on the road of how the goddess was certain to pity her and to restore her true self. He whispered to her that the goddess would once again match her inner beauty to her previous outer beauty.

The girl, however, had continued to maintain her silence behind the thick black veil, a deathly presence without a face floating silently through the even more silent forest.

The Minotaur assured the father that the great goddess would bless and heal his daughter. The gods could not be so cruel and so unjust.

The father nodded and thanked the monster for his kind words. They walked on in silence together, until the father smiled slightly and said:

You know, guardsman, after you and she are both healed by the goddess, perhaps you could marry each other. I do not want her marrying her old betrothed anymore, after he callously abandoned her. You seem noble in your character. My wine presses are far lovelier and richer than a little fabric shop in Knossos.

We will see. Let's just hope the goddess is kind to us all and looks kindly upon us in our unjust afflictions.

The two men walked further along, with the veiled girlish specter trailing behind. The girl continued to maintain her silence. The men occasionally offered comments to each other about the weather, or the sound of a darting little animal in the bush, or the odd lack of color in the dark, monotonous forest. Still, these comments were rare and led, at most, to an exchange of a few words back and forth. There were long stretches of silence when the forest's overhanging, tangled branches and foliage seemed to be suffocating the three isolated pilgrims with darkness and quiet.

As the sun was close to setting, the sounds started. These were not small animals, but footsteps, heavy and approaching from the left side of the road. The monster saw the glint of several daggers. Thieves (or worse) were falling upon them, and fast. The monster signaled to his two companions to be silent, and he led them up a tall nearby tree. With the help of the Minotaur's great muscles, the three reached the upper branches and hid themselves in the thick leaves.

The robber band passed by underneath and fanned out in a different direction. The Minotaur and the father agreed the little group should spend the night in the tree, just in case the robbers should circle back again. The girl made no comment, but adjusted herself on a wide branch to be more comfortable.

The father was the first one to fall asleep. The monster lay on his back and looked up through the few leaves over his head to the stars above. His mind drifted back to his bedchamber in Knossos and the comfort of the fake painted stars on his old ceiling. He longed for his mother's stroking hand on his cheek.

For the first time, the girl spoke to the monster:

Do you like the stars? I love the stars. I used to watch them back home from a small bridge. I know all the constellations.

Me too. Or I once knew them all. I have trouble remembering each constellation now.

What I love about the stars is how reliable they are. They don't grow old, die, get sick, become ugly, or change their minds about anything. They sit up there, calmly, beyond suffering and change, showing off their beauty, but keeping people at a safe distance. I wish I could be a star. Maybe make friends with Orion. We could have a star wedding together.

You could beseech the goddess Aphrodite to place your body up in the stars. I am sure that is within her power.

Very funny. I will be happy to be transformed into myself again.

She paused and her veil turned up to the sky. The girl continued in a more serious tone:

Do you think that the goddess will help us? Or are we fated to be monsters forever? I hate being a monster. I cannot live a real life and move forward. Being a monster means being stuck in the corner and never getting your rightful turn. It is not fair. I want to be a beautiful bride, and a mother, and to be able to walk proudly in the sunset. But now I cannot do any of these things. My mother says I am cursed to wander the temples begging for food, and that no man will ever touch a girl with a deformed face.

I know the goddess will help us. Twists of fate can be cruel, but the gods are ultimately just. The goddess will see your virtue and your goodness, and she will reward you.

I think it is harder for a girl to be a monster than for a boy to be a monster. You still have those big muscles. You maybe could work somewhere, like in a field where they could use your strength. Some girl would marry you, she would fall in love with those big muscles, and she would teach herself to love you despite your appearance. Girls can do that. We can learn to love someone by being with them every day and growing closer. But boys can't. If your face does not please a boy, no amount of goodness can change his heart. It is not fair.

That is not true. Maybe it will be harder and take longer, but a man will come around who will love you for your character and your wisdom. It is not all about being pretty.

You are wrong.

The girl paused.

I will only believe you if you look at my face without this veil, and promise me if the goddess rejects both of our prayers and leaves us as monsters, you will marry me. You say I have all these wonderful virtues. Well, brother monster look into my real face and promise me if we are both doomed to be monsters, you will be my monster husband and love me for my goodness and wisdom despite my face.

The girl sat up on her branch and leaned towards the Minotaur's bull head and horns. With her head now covering his whole line of sight and blocking out all the leaves and stars above, she removed her veil with a shaking hand.

The unveiled face was hideous. One of the eyes was twisted and slanted and no more than a burned out hollow socket. The lips were gone, as was half the nose. The cheeks were wrinkled and shrunk into innumerable little veins and clumps crisscrossing and colliding over the charred, brownish skin.

The monster, without thinking, turned his head away quickly and tightly shut his eyes. He could not bring himself to look at her. He knew he was being horribly cruel, he did not want to hurt her, but the sight of her was more than he could handle.

Promise me! Promise me now!

Liar.

She hit the monster, as hard as she could, with a tight fist. She exhausted herself landing her blows, which barely grazed the monster's powerful body.

Even you, a hideous ugly monster yourself, think you are too good for me. I hate you all.

The girl lay back on her branch, with her veil once again covering her face. Her muffled, stifled little sobs wafted up from below, and burned the monster's guilty conscience. He did not move and felt unable to forgive himself. The Minotaur kept his head down. He was ashamed to show himself to the stars. He knew he should say something, beg her forgiveness, but he could not bear the thought of seeing that monstrously deformed face again.

The girl's sobs eventually turned to snores, beaten down, defeated, monotonous snores. The monster slowly adjusted his position and sat up. He felt nothing but disgust with himself when he looked at the back of the veiled sleeping figure. He knew he could not continue traveling with these two companions. As they slept, he crept silently down the tree and resumed walking the road, by himself, to the goddess's shrine.

The monster felt he had failed an important test of his soul. And he wished more desperately than ever to abandon the world of the monsters.

He wanted the simplicity of being beautiful with other beautiful people, and all of the ugliness exiled to the far corners of the earth, hissing in a corner until some beautiful man should choose to play hero and to cut the ugliness out of existence. Then the world would be easy in its uninterrupted beauty.

VI. In the Sacred Grove of the Goddess Aphrodite

THE MONSTER AGAIN covered his head completely with his hood, so as not to arouse suspicion, he told himself; although it was unclear why he took this precaution given the deserted state of the forest. There was no one on the road.

There were fewer and fewer birds and no small animals in the bushes. Even the insects had apparently left this part of the forest. It was as if every living thing except the monster understood this was a place for the strongest of trees alone, and these trees would brook no interference with their secret, sacred rites. The trees themselves seemed to stare at him with disapproval. The Minotaur felt shunned and somehow guilty of some transgression against the angry trees. Or perhaps the trees wanted to punish him for his cruelty to a vulnerable, hopeful young girl.

The sun set. There was a pale, faint moon, which barely breached the dense wooded tangle overhead. The branches seemed to be reaching further into the road from the top and the sides. It was soon almost completely dark. The monster groped slowly along the road using a large fallen branch as a walking stick. His labored breathing and the gentle touch of his makeshift staff to the dirt were the only sounds. The absolute dark and the absolute quiet infused the Minotaur's soul with dread. It seemed to his disoriented mind that something must break the tension, and that something would have knife-like teeth or a shining sharp dagger.

The monster walked on in the pitch black silence. He went around one bend and then another. The road had become winding and was difficult to follow. He felt as if he were going downhill and descending into some sort of valley, but it was hard to be sure. As the monster fumbled through the descending turns, the branches grabbed and pricked and cut and tousled his arms and hands and legs and feet. He felt little drops of blood seep out of his skin and dry in stale little puddles on his sweaty flesh.

Past one particularly sharp turn the monster saw an amazing sight: up ahead, distant but visible, appeared to be candles brightly burning. He heard no sounds that would indicate there were any men or women near the candles. Nor were there any signs of human habitation. But the monster's spirits were uplifted by the surprising sight of the inviting orange yellow light. As the monster approached the lights, the forest became slowly visible again to him in the darkness. The dark branches formed a thick interlacing roof over the Minotaur's head. In the faint orange glow he could see their thickness and rough, bulging contours. They seemed old but strong. There were no hanging leaves or fruit. Even though it was summer, these trees seemed to inhabit a perpetual winter.

On the sides of the road the monster could make out wide tree trunks packed closely together forming something like a wall. It would be difficult to pass between them. And again, there were no leaves or fruits or flowers. He noticed the rotting carcass of a deer hanging from the branches of a tree on the side of the road, as if the angry barren branches had mauled the poor animal for sport. The monster felt that the eyes of the corpse seemed to be watching him.

The path sloped ever more sharply downward. There were no more curves. Rather, the monster felt like a rock rolling downhill by an unseen hand. The force of the pull down grew stronger as he went faster and faster. The light of the candles grew brighter and closer. The light seemed to have grabbed his hand and to be pulling the monster, relentlessly, into its orbit.

The Minotaur reached a level plateau. The trees to his left thinned out, and he could see a vast array of lanterns hung from branches and carefully set in rows on the ground. Through the lights there was a well-paved path made of glowing pink marble. In the distance, down the path, he thought he could make out a face carved into an old tree. The monster realized he had come to the grove of the great goddess Aphrodite.

His heart beat quickly with anticipation. The monster told himself he was on the brink of salvation. He had finally arrived at the goddess's abode. She would surely hear his supplication and take pity on his wounded heart. She would feel sorrow for the forlorn, abandoned lover and give to the Minotaur the metamorphosis necessary to win his beloved Ariadne.

He walked down the brightly lit path. The candles gave off a powerful fragrance, similar to incense, but sweeter and lighter. The side of this marble path was strewn with high bushes bursting with colorful flowers whose scents mixed with the candles' smell. The tree branches also came to life: There were soft leaves and ripe, glowing fruits directly above the monster's head and across from his shoulders. After the steep descent through the tunnel of barren wintry dark trees, the grove's warm colors and scents brought forth in the monster a wild, bursting feeling of being alive. The Minotaur experienced a sudden and dizzying romantic infatuation with the world around him.

The monster felt as if he was floating along the path. Everything appeared easy to him. It was as if the trees and flowers were gently encouraging and reassuring him. The monster told himself the gods had seen his unjust suffering and were reaching out with kind arms to cradle and rock him. He loved and he thought that he was loved in turn by the world surrounding him.

The path abruptly ended at a grove of trees. Lanterns hung from the branches of these trees. The trees were short, not much taller than the monster, and filled with thick, fragrant leaves. The lanterns were positioned to illuminate great carved faces in the tree trunks. The monster was not sure if the light was for him to see the faces or for the faces to see him. Each face was a woman, a beautiful woman, but a different woman, as if the artist had set himself the task of creating a gallery of portraits of archetypal female beauty. The workmanship was extraordinary: The faces were perfectly lifelike in every detail. The faces were brightly and carefully painted. The skins were a range of hues as were the hair, eyes, and lips. The eyes were all wide open. There was something intense about the stares in each set of eyes. Each seemed alive and waiting.

The monster could see, dimly, past the grove, an altar and shrine and statues. That must be the abode of the priests, he thought. He was almost there. He just needed to pass this grove of carved wooden faces, and then he would kneel at the altar and offer his prayer to the goddess. With the morning light the priests would come, and the monster was certain the goddess would have told them in their dreams of his plight. They would come to the prostrate Minotaur by the altar already knowing their instructions. He would be healed, and he would be remade as a beautiful man.

The monster walked into the grove of trees. The trees were arranged in a circle with the carved and painted faces in the trunks all staring towards the center. As he stepped into that center of the grove, the Minotaur heard a whispered command:

Halt.

The monster stopped. He waited. Hearing nothing further the monster decided it was the wind playing tricks upon his excited mind. But when he started to move again the same whisper commanded:

Halt.

The voice now sounded harsher, even annoyed with his disobedience. The voice continued:

Kneel in supplication.

The monster obeyed this time without hesitation. The voice had become gentler again, but was still firm. He could not discern from which direction the voice came. Its sound was metallic and clear, but seemed to surround the monster in every direction. He looked up after he kneeled down. It seemed to the monster that the faces on the trees were boring into his soul with their eyes. He felt penetrated, prodded, poked, and jostled; although he was perfectly still and there was no one there. There were no sounds besides the voice in the air.

Time slowed to a stop. The monster was shaking and his eyes searched the ground to avoid the harsh stares from the faces on the trees. Eventually, the poking seemed to lessen, or else the monster became accustomed to it. He breathed more easily.

The voice came again, firm but soft:

State your business before the great goddess Aphrodite.

The Minotaur bent his head to the ground. He inhaled deeply. Then the monster uttered his prayer:

Oh great goddess Aphrodite, heavenly queen of love and beauty, bringer of the sweet fruits of desire and the hard bitter taste of heartbreak and longing, I, your humble servant, have come here to beseech your blessing and your grace. I was born a deformed monster from the womb of my mother, who was stricken with a fatal passion for a white bull. I have the body and soul of a man, but the monstrous, grotesque head of a bull. Because of my curse my parents hid me from my fellow men. Through my own clever devices, I met a beautiful girl, a true devotee of yours, whom I loved. But she did not return my love. She spurned me cruelly and laughed at my love for her. I fled my home after that terrible ordeal, and I have traveled to this sacred place.

As the great goddess must see in her wisdom, I have known terrible pain and heartbreak. As long as I am trapped in the form of a monster I cannot partake in the world of love. I am doomed to be either a violent beast, upon whom terrible revenge must be exacted someday, or a ridiculous silly fool pretending to seek human love when no pretty girl could imagine herself kissing my lips. A monster can only be a target of the hero's righteous rage or a pitiful farce. But I wish to be the hero, to save and embrace my beloved and to be a good husband and father. I wish to play different roles than the ones assigned to me unjustly at my birth. I am a noble and virtuous soul, great goddess. I abound in love and courage and kindness. Please hear the pleading of your humble servant, heal his pain, and transform him into a man, fully a man, and let him taste the sweetness of a love returned.

The monster's body shook after these words poured out of him and he shed hot, flowing tears, uncontrollably. The tears flooded the monster's eyes, and he could not see clearly. His head ached and spun around. He fell further towards the ground. The monster was terrified. The goddess's judgment would soon be upon him.

The voice returned, hard and mocking:

The poor, sad, weeping Minotaur wishes to be a dashing and handsome lover. His heart breaks. He cannot bear the yoke of his fate. He cannot live as a monster. He must be beautiful and even be a hero. He longs for the gods to save him from what he is, to remake him as a handsome man who could wed lovely Ariadne. The Minotaur does not wish to take his place in the annals of the immortal monsters, great terrible beasts that inspire fear and terror in the hearts of men and rouse the souls of brave heroes to wondrous deeds. No, the Minotaur wants to change the script written by fate, to ask the great goddess to reconsider whether the plans of the gods are, in this case, too cruel or too unjust or maybe mistaken.

Know monstrous beast that your birth was a just and fitting punishment to King Minos and Queen Pasiphae. In his wars, King Minos had desecrated temples and shrines and failed to respect and honor the gods. Queen Pasiphae impiously refused to live as a human queen to her husband. She wished, of all absurd things, to be a stupid cow whose only purpose was to be fattened for the slaughter. She used magic to try to undo the work and intentions of the gods. Both Minos and Pasiphae displayed a deep, and unforgiveable, arrogance. Both of them refused to submit to the will of the gods and to honor the gods. So they were marked for a curse: They would have no human child, but only one offspring, a hideous, repellant monster, who would be a source of shame. Eventually a great hero would arise in Athens who would travel to Knossos and slay the loathsome monster. It would become one of this hero's great deeds, about which poets would sing forever after.

But the Minotaur himself now refuses to bend to the gods' will. He does not believe he is well suited for the life of a monster. He does not wish to inspire terror. Nor does he wish to be a test for a great hero. He dreams of marrying pretty Ariadne and working the wine press in the countryside. The Minotaur wishes to be erased from the poets' grand song of valor and great deeds, and to fade into the background of insignificant, forgotten little men who while away their days.

The Minotaur is not the first monster to question his fate and to make demands upon the great gods. The terrible Cyclops Polyphemos lost his heart to Galatea, the beautiful nymph. She did not return the love of the wretched, ugly one-eyed brute. The Cyclops begged the gods for mercy, even wished that a stranger would come and poke out his one eye so the sight of Galatea would no longer torture his soul. The gods answered his prayer in part: He stayed a monster, the pain of his longing for Galatea was never soothed, but the gods will send a stranger, a great traveling hero, through the waves one day to visit Polyphemos in his cave to burn his eye out with a hot poker. Polyphemos is a monster, and he will only be permitted the life and sufferings of a monster. It was not his place to sink into tender caresses and to recite heartfelt love songs. The lovely nymph Galatea knew this too, and she would always spurn that repulsive, deformed one-eyed face and give her favors only to the bronzed fishermen with faces as pretty as her own.

The Minotaur, too, shall submit to the will of the gods. There shall be no change to his fate. He was born a monster, he will live a monster's fate, and he will be remembered as a monster. The Minotaur's pitiable whims and laments are of no concern to the gods. The Minotaur shall be returned to Knossos, imprisoned, and, at the appointed hour, killed by the hero chosen for immortal fame.

The voice stopped speaking. There were no further sounds of any kind.

The monster refused to believe there was no hope. There must be a way, he told himself. He felt a sudden surge of rage course through him. This simply could not be his fate. The Minotaur raised his head and demanded justice:

But why must this be so, great goddess Aphrodite? Whatever sins may have been committed by Queen Pasiphae and King Minos, let the gods punish them. What have I done? I have hurt no one. I have tried to be pious and upright. I have done nothing to deserve imprisonment or a cruel death. I do not want to sew fear in anyone's heart. I want the men and women around me to see there is nothing to fear, that I am kind and good and pious. Why? Why? This cannot be. I refuse to believe it.

The monster stood up, his body shaking, but around him was only silence. The night had grown darker and the light of the candles in the lanterns on the trees seemed dimmer. The monster looked into the silent painted faces carved into the trees. He thought he could see them smirking. They were laughing at him, he thought, in their silent, arrogant way. He felt angrier. The Minotaur could not accept the injustice of the great goddess's judgment.

In his indignant fury the monster lowered his horns and charged at one of the faces. He was thrown to the ground. He got up again and charged another face. Again, he was thrown to the ground. Again and again he charged, and again and again he was tossed down.

At a certain point in this futile brawl the monster took a hard fall from which he could not rise up again. He saw nothing but blackness. The blackness surrounded him, touched him, and then it devoured him. He was falling into the blackness. The monster could not feel any of his limbs, and he could not see anything. He could not wake from this blackness.

VII. The Monster is Captured
by the King's Men

WHEN THE MONSTER awoke he found himself in a bright open field. His hands and feet were bound tightly with coarse ropes, although someone had meticulously dressed and stitched the many cuts, bruises, and abrasions that pockmarked his body. The monster looked up and saw there were armed men everywhere. By the crest on their shields these men were recognizable as palace guards for King Minos.

Where am I? the Minotaur called out.

The armed men ignored him. They were split into different groups telling jokes or playing games of dice. It was uncertain whether they did not hear the Minotaur, or if they just did not care to answer him.

The monster tried again: Where am I? Why have I been tied up?

The same continual laughing and murmuring conversations. But this time, at least, the monster's cries drew a few responsive cries of shut up and be quiet.

He sat up as best he could and looked around. There were some hastily raised canvas tents nearby, clearly the soldiers' temporary quarters. Someone had started a fire and appeared to be cooking a meal; some kind of meat was burning. The smell of roasting fatty meat made the strictly vegetarian monster feel nauseous. There was an old woman to the side washing clothes in a large basin and doing some mending. She hummed a song to herself. The monster could not make out what it was.

Another man exited one of the tents. By his uniform he was an officer of some kind. He came right over to the monster. He was a middle-aged man, surprisingly portly for a member of the palace guards, with an inviting grin and a bristly but full blue black beard. He was bald on top, but had some matching blue black hair on the sides of his head. He had no weapons or shield. The man sat down next to the Minotaur, uncomfortably close. The monster thought this man looked relaxed and even upbeat:

Well, I am glad to see you are up. Those were some nasty sores and cuts on your hide. You are lucky we found you and could get you some medical attention before the wounds festered and some piece of you may have been necessary to amputate. But I think it will heal alright now. You need to stay off the left leg for a while, it got cut up worse than your other parts. Walking will only aggravate the wounds. I will give you a draught to ease the pain. Try to rest, though.

My apologies for the ropes binding you. We need to be sure you do not run off again. And why should you? Look at how you fared out there in the world. It would only be a matter of time before some angry man or rabid animal did you in for good. You are fortunate we found you first. Why you would run away from the world's most elegant and lovely palace, where you were royalty, to run around a forest like a savage, is beyond my understanding. Nevertheless, you will be home very soon. We pull up camp tomorrow morning.

The man stood up before the monster could ask any further questions, went back into his tent, and came out with a jar with a clear, thick liquid that smelled of soap. The man walked briskly back over to the monster and poured the liquid down his throat. The Minotaur was too startled to do anything but acquiesce. Soon the monster felt himself losing all sensation in his body, and his head seemed to float. He found it hard to concentrate on any of his thoughts. Light-headed and numb, he drifted in and out of a thin sleep.

As the monster would later learn, the man with whom he had spoken was the physician for this particular regiment of the palace guards. After King Minos realized that the monster had fled the palace, search parties were sent to scour all of Crete. No one, however, could find him. Rumors circulated that the Minotaur was dead. Sometimes some crazy peasant swore he had seen the monster with the fearsome bull's head up in a tree, but no one believed him. For a time the king had given up the search.

Queen Pasiphae was beside herself with sorrow. She went into mourning and would see no one. Guards were posted at her bedside to make sure that, in her despair, she did nothing rash, such as jumping out of a window or driving a dagger into her breast. Physicians in the royal household were called upon more than once to examine her to reassure His Majesty that the queen was eating sufficiently and there were no signs of attempted self-administration of poison.

One morning, however, an officious-looking, pot-bellied priest, wrapped sloppily in a wrinkled crimson robe loosely cinched at the waist, barged into the palace and demanded an immediate audience with the king and queen. This fellow—who was quite out of breath from running up the palace steps—was from the temple of Aphrodite in Knossos. He would speak to no one but the king and queen, and claimed to have an urgent message from the great goddess Aphrodite herself.

After much debate among the offended court officials about this importunate gate-crasher's failure to respect proper court protocol, King Minos and Queen Pasiphae agreed to receive him. After all, a message from a goddess was not to be ignored, no matter how rude or rumpled the messenger might be. The priest was ushered into a small reception room with two guards flanking him. The king and queen entered through a different door on the other side of the room and sat down. One of the guards instructed the priest to prostrate himself and to state his business.

The priest said he had come to relay his dream of the previous night. Indeed, the matter was clearly so urgent he came right to the palace upon waking, hardly even bothering to dress himself properly. In his dream, the priest was sitting in the great goddess Aphrodite's sacred grove in the forest on the western mountain, surrounded by the many smiling faces of the goddess carved into the trees. He was eating some bread and drinking wine, and the day was sunny and clear. Suddenly, one of the faces called to him and then left her tree and floated over to him. No body, just a head, floating through the air. The head went to the priest and whispered into his ear: The escaped monster of King Minos, the hideous Minotaur, has come to my shrine. As soon as you awake, tell this message to King Minos and Queen

Pasiphae, but only to them directly: I will leave the monster for the king's troops to capture in a field near my shrine, but the king must move with dispatch to bring his monster back to the royal palace. Once the Minotaur has returned to Knossos he must be locked up securely, so that there are no further escapes.

Queen Pasiphae wept for joy, quietly, and smiled at this vision. Her beloved son was alive and would come home. She did not, however, think too deeply as of yet about the goddess's command to ensure the monster was imprisoned in the palace without a chance of escape. To the contrary, she ordered her household to clean and dust her son's bedchamber, and to make sure his favorite foods were well stocked in the pantry.

King Minos summoned a commander of a regiment of the palace guards, and ordered him and his company to march to the shrine that morning. For the time being, the mission was to be kept secret; King Minos did not wish to alarm his subjects about a monster on the loose.

The guards began the march, as they typically do, laughing and jostling and bragging and storytelling. But as they traveled deeper into the forest, and the sun's light was blocked more and more by black branches without leaves, their chatter dissipated, and a tense quiet swept over the marching regiment. Silent prayers were mumbled to favorite gods (none of whom were the great goddess of love, Aphrodite, much to her divine chagrin. The goddess of love and beauty was not viewed as useful by men who fought for a living).

The guards encountered a horribly deformed leper begging by the side of the road, with lumps growing all over his once human face and hands deformed into claws. Blood trickled from his nose all over the ground, so that he sat in a big puddle of his own dried blood. He begged for food, wine, and alms; he said the goddess had abandoned and scorned him, although he had done no wrong; he offered to sing sweet songs for the soldiers, songs that would remind them of childhood. The leper claimed that, before his affliction, he was beloved by all the children in his village. It would be a blessing if these good men would give him a chance to brighten the gloomy forest with his songs.

The soldiers recoiled at the sight of this hideous roadside monster. Seeing that his pleas were spurned by men as well as gods, the leper became desperate. He lunged for the nearest soldier to grab his boots and to prostrate himself. The leper succeeded in grabbing a boot and penetrating a circle of guards. The march slowed. The soldier whom the leper had grabbed tried to free himself from the monstrous man's mad claw-like grip, but could not. A comrade of his drew a sword and ran the leper through the back. The guards did not desire to touch the wretched diseased body, so they kicked the corpse to the side of the road with their boots. They left the leper's corpse exposed to rot where it lay and moved on.

The company was even more somber after this incident with the gruesome leper. They wanted to complete their task and leave the cursed, dark forest road as soon as possible. Thus, there were great sighs of relief and muted cheers when one of the guards saw the Minotaur snoring on a field to the side of the road, as if he were waiting for the regiment of guards to come and pick him up.

After the regiment's physician had checked on his bound monster patient and given him the strong drink to numb his pain, the physician walked away and went to speak to two tallish men who wore more ornate helmets than the others. These were the commanding officers of the regiment. The three men entered a tent and consulted with each other in private.

Soon there was a great deal of movement. The tents were coming down. Six men soon stood and hovered over the monster. None of them looked at his face. One of these men gave hand signals to the others; the waiting group lifted the Minotaur onto a small litter with a wooden floor and wooden roof. The sides of the litter were composed of thick black wool curtains. No prying eyes of passersby would be able to penetrate the dark veil of the curtains.

The monster lay on the ground in the litter for some time. There were all sorts of shouts and orders and directives, which were answered with a chorus of perfunctory assents or muttered curses. At some point the litter was raised and the monster was carried along, still drifting between sleep and alertness. It was a horrendous ride. The air in the litter was stifling in its heat and humidity and the stale odors of the monster's sweat. The litter was often jostled. The monster became nauseous and begged the guards to stop marching and to put him down. He was told to shut up. He vomited. The guards did not care and chose to let the Minotaur lay in his vomit.

The men carrying the monster were quite strong and went some distance without a break. When the procession did stop for a rest, the monster was, without warning, dropped to the ground. The swift fall and banging against the hard wood floor sent waves of searing pain through his bruised body. A hand slipped under the dark side curtain and gave him a thick bag of leaves and a jug of water. He refreshed himself and even had a little water left over to clean the vomit from his body.

The monster eventually fell asleep again and lost track of time and his surroundings. The guards marched swiftly and silently. To a man, they wished to escape the grim forest road cursed with lepers and other monsters. The guards sometimes passed farmers or shepherds or servant girls in the countryside, but answered their greetings with grunts and cold flinty eyes.

One overly friendly farmer did not follow the meaning of those hard icy eyes shooting out from under the guards' helmets. He would not stop insisting that the guards stop and sample his freshly pressed wine. A hand grabbed the man's cloak and threw him down, hard, to the side of the road. He stumbled up, with cuts bleeding on his forehead. He massaged his sore arm that had collided with a stone on the ground and walked away, not understanding why the guards from the great city were so rude.

VIII. Into the Labyrinth

WHEN THE MINOTAUR awoke next he found himself in a strange room, which he did not recognize. On the walls were pictures of battles—elongated men with curly beards driving chariots and spears at one another. Some of the men were dead; others were dropping, wounded in battle. The pigments were foreboding: the men and weapons and horses and chariots were in browns and blacks; the only color was a dark red for the blood. The room was dark. There were no windows. The only lights were dim yellow torches placed in notches scattered sparsely along the walls.

The monster had been laid in a bed. It was wooden and hard, with a coarse tan covering—like something a soldier would carry on a march. He yawned and rubbed the fog of sleep from his eyes. There were four soldiers in the room guarding him. When they saw that the monster was awake, one of them exited. He returned several minutes later with the regimental physician, who waved a warm hello and examined the monster's wounds, sores, and lesions. Once he completed his inspection of the lower, bruised human body parts, the physician walked towards where the monster's great bull head lay. The monster looked up at him. He seemed to the monster to be a big floating smile, drifting like a cloud in the room.

The Minotaur felt heavy and dull. He wanted to find some way to sleep more; he did not enjoy the sensation of wakefulness any longer. The monster patiently waited for the physician to speak.

Your wounds look much better. They have healed well. You still need to be careful, do not do any strenuous athletic exercises yet, but I think you will be fine. I am going to let the king know you have recovered.

With a happy bounce in his step, the physician waved goodbye and left the room without waiting for any response.

The monster stared blankly at the soldiers. He did not feel like moving. He did not want to do anything but somehow, some way, lose consciousness again. The Minotaur was drained of all desire.

New guards entered; the shift had changed. Someone brought the monster fresh grass and water. He ate slowly, but not much.

The monster studied the men painted on the walls. Their faces were sketched without much detail. Nevertheless their expressions still conveyed a feeling of earnest, manly fighting. These men were intent on what they were doing. They appeared convinced that their war, whatever it was, was important and worth a great deal of courage and thought and effort. This struck the monster as ridiculous, and he laughed softly under his breath. What was the point of all this clashing of chariots and shields? The dice were no doubt loaded, and the victor already predetermined by the gods.

The monster wondered when he was going to be returned to the care of his mother, the queen, in her comfortable tower. He was tired of the labored friendliness of the physician. He longed for his mother's warm smile and her ample servings of finely seasoned grass.

Lost in these daydreams, the monster did not notice the door swing open again. An immense troop of guards filed in followed by attendants wearing elaborately embroidered robes. The final member of this procession was Daedalus, court chamberlain to King Minos.

Daedalus was not a happy man. He was short and thin, the ferret-like runt of the Cretan nobility, and chosen for his position among Crete's nobles because he was the man other men could least imagine replacing Minos as king of the island. Daedalus was left in charge of Crete during Minos's foreign wars, and it was his responsibility in the king's absence to dole out justice among bickering local lords. However, no matter what he did with any well-reasoned and well-supported arguments, Minos, upon returning home, would provide some gift for the losing party and commiserate about

Daedalus's foolish and unjust decision. While this tactic helped to consolidate Minos's popularity, it left Daedalus feeling betrayed each time. He would beg the king to relieve him of his duties, citing the king's own comments about Daedalus's incompetence. But King Minos would insist Daedalus remain at his post to continue to judge disputes in the king's absence.

The latest unpleasant job that King Minos handed to Daedalus was to carry through the command of Aphrodite that the Minotaur somehow be securely locked up, so there would be no future escapes. Given the monster's all too easy flight from the queen's tower, there was no question of him living with his mother again. So Daedalus was told that he, and he alone, was responsible for finding some new way to contain the monster.

Daedalus met with the king's engineers to craft a plan. It was decided that a prison cell would not work, as the monster could break the lock or overpower the guard at feeding time. Moreover, the sight of the monster sitting sadly in his cage, longing for his mother or his freedom, might elicit meddlesome sympathy.

So Daedalus pondered the situation further, and studied the designs and plans of the palace complex until he hit upon what he was sure was a brilliant idea: bringing the labyrinth back into use. The labyrinth was an underground dungeon beneath the main palace building that King Minos's predecessors had used to torture their enemies to death. The condemned man would be drugged and taken into the heart of the pitch black labyrinth. He would awaken to complete silence, darkness, and isolation. The man would rise and try to find a way out, but would inevitably become lost in the labyrinth's winding, twisting passageways. The prisoner would begin to lose his sanity; soon he would die horribly from hunger, thirst, self-inflicted wounds, or bites from the rats—or some mixture of the four. No one, reputedly, had ever escaped the labyrinth. So the labyrinth seemed to Daedalus to be a perfect solution: The monster would be penned in, and no one would need to see him.

Daedalus realized, however, that his plan to imprison the Minotaur in the labyrinth was not without its problems. King Minos had sworn an oath to the great god Poseidon when the monster was born to safeguard him. So the monster, unlike the previous prisoners, had to survive in the labyrinth. Daedalus worked with the palace engineers to build a pipe from a nearby well into the center of the labyrinth, so that the monster could pump fresh water. The engineers designed and built a pulley system to pass down food and candles and oil for the wicks (as the total darkness of the labyrinth could have ill effects on the monster's mental health). Once these renovations were complete, Daedalus waited for the physician to report that the monster was safe to transport to his new underground home.

Daedalus paced back and forth at the foot of the monster's makeshift bed in silence. Every so often he would stop and appear to make mental notes to himself. He cleared his throat a couple of times. The guards watched him, first nervously, but then with growing impatience. They found the nervous and self-important rodent-like little man to be tiresome in his circling and swaying about the bed. Feeling the increasingly irritated stares of the guards, Daedalus stopped pacing the room and addressed the monster in a high-pitched nasal voice:

You gave us all quite a fright. You have no idea how worried and heartbroken your mother was. She rent her clothes and moaned and would see no one. We had all thought you had been killed, or had killed yourself, or had gone mad. You are lucky we tracked you down. Your travels on the forest highway were not the safest activity. You are a monster, try to re-member, and outside of King Minos's gracious protection there are many who would take aim at your head.

We will never understand why you fled from the palace. King Minos has always clothed and fed and coddled and guarded you. Despite the dis-gusting manner of your conception and birth, you have lived the life of a member of the royal family. Your selfishness and lack of gratitude are truly disappointing.

But that is in the past. The king must look to the future. We cannot let you run free. For your own safety you must be penned in somewhere. There is a suite of apartments underneath the palace known as the palace labyrinth. It is a dark confusing maze of winding and circling hallways and corridors. It was built several generations back to torture traitors. Rather than dying a clean easy death, the traitor would be sent into the dark laby-rinth. The condemned man would lose his mind, alone and lost in the darkness, desperately seeking some escape. Most of these men succumbed to madness and bashed their skulls out against the walls.

You will sojourn in the labyrinth. However, you will not be harmed. King Minos has promised the great god Poseidon to keep you safe, and the royal house of Crete keeps its oaths to the great gods. Under my supervision, the king's engineers have had the labyrinth renovated somewhat, and you will be able to live out your days there comfortably and peaceably. These loyal guards and I are here to escort you to your new home.

Daedalus clasped his hands together behind his back once he had finished speaking. He looked up at the ceiling and judged his speech to have been excellent. He felt that he had, once more, executed the king's command in an exemplary manner. Of course, he thought, should anything go wrong, should this beast somehow escape ...

I wish to see my mother.

Daedalus was not expecting this request from the monster. He had assumed the monster would do as monsters do: acquiesce to overwhelming force or try to fight his way out. Daedalus was not sure what to say. He stared at his fingernails and nodded his head silently. Without looking up, he heaved a deep sigh and brushed this request aside:

I am afraid that is not in your best interest or the queen's. You upset her greatly with your flight. Her nerves are still fragile. Seeing you would only upset her and make the necessary transition to the labyrinth harder on you. Let us look to the future and to your time underground as a time to nurture and grow. Like a fine glistening white mushroom, I am sure you will grow strong and noble in the dark subterranean air.

Daedalus decided it was time to get this task over and done with. He was not comfortable engaging in further conversation with a menacing, terrible bull's head. Daedalus signaled the guards behind him with his hand. The monster was helped out of bed. He was uneasy on his feet from having been confined for so long to bed rest. The monster did not try to insist any further on seeing his mother, or anything else. He appeared to have no will of his own left.

The procession of Daedalus, Minotaur, attendants, and guards went through one hallway after another, down various staircases, and through yet more hallways. The monster let himself be led without any resistance. He was quiet, as were his many escorts. The Minotaur paid no attention to the paintings on the wall.

The group wound their way to a far corner of the palace complex. They came to a lengthy underground stairwell and descended. The passageway was narrow, but the steps were surprisingly wide. It was clear the builder had not intended for anyone to trip. The walls were bare. The only light was a torch carried by the soldier at the front.

They stopped at a level landing. There was a large stone archway with a high ceiling. Daedalus instructed the soldiers to light additional torches. He also instructed three soldiers to remove balls of yarn from a bag he carried. There was a post in front of the archway. Each soldier tied one end of his ball of yarn to the post. The group entered the labyrinth. The soldiers unraveled their yarn as they went; that was clearly the method for finding one's way securely in and out of the dark underground maze.

Nonetheless, Daedalus seemed to know his way. The procession snaked around the corridors, now this way, now that way, until they came to what Daedalus confidently pronounced to be the center of the labyrinth. Here the group arrived at a finely furnished living space for the monster. There were three adjacent rooms with connecting doors: a bedroom; a chamber pot; and a study. The rooms were small. There were notches in the walls for oil lamps. Next to the bed were several chests containing scrolls (picked by the royal librarian from his memory of the Minotaur's more frequent borrowings), bags of leaves, and changes of clothes. Against the wall were several barrels of wine. The chamber pot had a lever to empty its contents into a deep pit far below the labyrinth. Daedalus proudly assured the assembled crowd that the monster would never have to worry about the smell wafting back up.

In the study there was a dumbwaiter, which was quite large. Daedalus explained that food, wine, candles, and other provisions would be sent down to the monster. The monster nodded absentmindedly through this entire presentation. He was calm and docile. Daedalus finally tired of explicating his many ingenious improvements to the labyrinth. As soon as he stopped lecturing the group, the guards wasted no time in exiting the labyrinth, using the unraveled yarn to guide their way, and pulling the tiresome Daedalus along with them.

When the Minotaur was finally alone in his new home, he lay back on the bed and stared at the darkness. Sleep came slowly and without the monster's full awareness. The Minotaur had no worries. There were no beauties here to love without being loved in return, no men or beasts to threaten him, nothing at all to do but drift and float. The monster's soul emptied itself.

Time passed differently in the labyrinth. There was no way to delineate night from day. The Minotaur's body made its own time and calendar. At a certain point the monster felt ready, on his own unconscious clock, to rise out of his stupor. He stretched his limbs, ate a quick meal, lit a lamp, and began to explore. The monster decided to use the same trick with the yarn that he saw Daedalus employ. He took one of his cloaks and tore it into thin strips and tied them together. The monster tied one end of the improvised fabric rope to one of his bed posts and carried the other in his hand as he went out to explore the labyrinth.

At first the labyrinth was terrifying to the monster. He jumped at every sound. There was a whole colony of small underground animals burrowing away somewhere, and they did not care if their busy errand-running kicked up an occasional racket in the dark passageways. But the Minotaur quickly realized there was nothing harmful in the labyrinth. While the hallways twisted and turned constantly, the monster began to notice a pattern: They all led back to the center, where his rooms were—except two. One led to the archway through which he had originally come. The other led to a back wall.

The Minotaur studied this back wall at length. There were, after all, precious few distractions in the labyrinth. He noticed there was an area where a rectangle was faintly outlined through slight indentures in the wall's otherwise flat plain. The monster pushed hard on the rectangle, and it gave way. He found himself staring into a hidden tunnel behind the wall. Even though the rectangle itself was not large—about the size of the monster's torso—the tunnel it concealed was quite high and wide.

The monster climbed through the opening and entered the tunnel. This tunnel appeared to have been constructed by the same builders as the labyrinth itself. It had clean stone walls and floors and ceilings. There were several ledges on the wall for holding torches. He walked on.

A little ways down the tunnel there was a sliver of sunlight. As the monster approached it grew larger, but fragmented into variously angled beams of light. He found himself at the end of the tunnel in front of an old wooden door, which was punctured by many holes, the source of the ricocheting sunbeams. The sight and feel of the sunlight pained his eyes, which had grown accustomed to the dark. Still, the monster felt a sudden exhilaration. He sat for some time by the door, enjoying the sun and learning to appreciate the light again.

After his eyes adjusted, the monster poked his head slightly out of the tunnel. He saw a familiar sight: the lovely palace gardens of Knossos. The door apparently led to a corner of the gardens behind a thick grove of trees. The Minotaur wondered if perhaps this was a secret passage built to smuggle prisoners out of the labyrinth. Or to go in and kill them? Either way, the trees and bushes in front of the door were so thick that it was quite well hidden.

Once he was certain that the sun had set, the monster returned to his bed chamber. He donned a dark cloak with a large hood and returned to the door; he exited into the palace gardens. The monster stayed close to the garden walls, so as to remain concealed. He snaked across the walls and through the hedges, slowly, quietly, until he came to the bottom of the garden-facing wall of Queen Pasiphae's tower.

The great fig tree still stood where he remembered it. The monster climbed the familiar branches and glided into his old bed chamber window. The room had remained untouched since he had left; it was a museum of his cozy boyhood. The monster looked up at the painted stars on the ceiling, where he once used to outline constellations with his sleepy fingers waving in the air. He thought to himself that this room was never dark, but always lit by the stars.

The Minotaur walked into the adjacent room, his mother's bedchamber. She was lying on the bed. She looked horrible: She was emaciated and pale, her cheeks were sunken, and wrinkles had proliferated around her body. Her hair was grey and tangled; she had clearly stopped coloring it. Queen Pasiphae stared out distantly at a wall. She was alone. There was one candle burning on her vanity. Her breathing was measured.

The monster approached his mother, the queen. She raised her head to him. She did not look alarmed or scared, but perplexed. Who was this visitor? How did he sneak up on her? She looked at her son like he was a perfume bottle that had been strangely left in the wrong place.

The Minotaur pulled his hood down. Her eyes lit up with life. She grabbed his hands and pulled him close. Mother and monster sat together silently, holding hands. She stroked his bull's cheek. After a pause, she spoke:

But how can you be here? You are a prisoner in the labyrinth.

The prison has its pores, and I can slip through them when I please.

Where will you go? King Minos will find you here. Have you planned your escape? Leave Crete. You must start over somewhere new. Somewhere kinder.

I will stay where I am. I will return to the labyrinth. My fate will follow me wherever I may travel; I cannot escape what I am. But I have longed to see you. Your touch is soft and a great comfort. Do not be sad.

I was so worried when you left. I kept imagining the terrible things Minos's men would do to you. I know you are no fighter. You have your father's gentle bearing. I woke every night from terrible dreams. I saw your head cut off and paraded around the palace walls. I wanted to hold you and protect you, but I could not. Every person I saw in the palace seemed somehow complicit in what, I was sure, was your murder. I bolted myself in this tower and gave myself up to grief. Then I heard you had been captured, and I thought my boy was coming home to me at long last. But King Minos—or, I should say, one of his messengers—told me I could not see you, as it would damage the fragile recovery of the queen's health. The next thing I heard was that you were to be imprisoned in the hideous labyrinth, and I could not bear it. I saw you going mad and smashing your skull to pieces against the walls, dying so horribly. My heart broke all over again. I prayed to the gods for death. I am too weak and cowardly to do the deed myself, but I thought maybe Minos would finally decide he had had enough of me. Maybe he would dispatch a guard to deliver a sword to my belly one evening …. But now you are here again, dear child. Please, stay with me as long as you can.

I will.

Thus mother and monster sat in the bed, holding each other, swaying and silent, until the dawn peaked out of the sky. The monster bid goodnight to his mother and slipped back down the tree, into the palace gardens, and through the secret door back into the labyrinth. The monster went to bed that morning feeling a warm tingling in his body.

The monster visited his mother regularly. He avoided visiting too frequently, as he did not want to be discovered. The Minotaur usually saw her twice a week, sometimes three or four times; it was hard for him to keep track of days and weeks in the pitch black of the labyrinth. Many nights the two sat together silently for hours, holding hands and rocking softly. Sometimes the monster's mother told him stories of her past and her thoughts. The monster, on the other hand, never spoke of his failed pilgrimage to the goddess Aphrodite, or of his failed love for Ariadne. The Minotaur had no wish to think of his past, but concentrated all his thoughts instead on a tender squeeze of the hand and the light, easy touch of the moonlight.

One evening, as the monster sneaked across the garden walls, he caught sight, through an open window, of a group of girls. They seemed to be seeking advice from each other. On this particular night, one of the girls stood in the middle of the circle and posed in many different ways with her dress and hair. She looked anxiously at her friends for their opinions—sometimes leading to smiles of delight, sometimes to indignant despair, but the reactions were always excessive. The monster watched them drowsily in the twilight. He wondered if they were planning to go to a palace ball or dinner party of some kind. Perhaps the girl in despair was upset because nothing she could do would catch the eye of the boy she loved. Or her mother was compelling her to wear a dress she loathed, and her friends had just confirmed her worst fears about the absurd figure that she struck.

It all seemed charming and amusing, harmless in a delightful way, until there she was: The next girl in the middle of the circle, prancing melodramatically until she collapsed into giggles, was Ariadne, lovely, petite, graceful Ariadne. She seemed utterly unchanged by her last, wretched evening with the monster. He thought to himself that it was as if she had never known him. It was a terrible shock to the Minotaur to be forced to admit to himself that he had been an irrelevant, albeit colorful, episode in her life. He had run off to secure a reprieve from the gods to win her love, which had been everything to him. She, on the other hand, had shrugged her shoulders and moved on.

The sight of her broke the monster's heart again. Looking at Ariadne gave him a feeling of sweet lightheadedness tinged with sadness and regret. He wanted to sit next to her again, to have their knees touch on a bench and to listen once more to the charming nightingale song of her chatter. Even though the monster knew she would marry another, he could not stop hoping for a few moments of being near her. That was all he still desired: proximity, to be next to her and to inhale her, a brief interlude where he could feel the delusion of being close to lovely Ariadne.

The monster stayed and stared through her whole performance before her friends. At the end he saw cheers, laughter, and smiles. Ariadne must have been a success. She would surely be admired, feted even, at the night's celebration, whatever it might be. The monster cowered in the night shadows and stared, trying not to be discovered, but feeling unable to stop himself from looking at her.

Ariadne left the pedestal and melted back into the crowd of friends. The Minotaur struggled to keep watching her, but she was no longer visible. He stared through the window for a long time, hoping, imagining, that she would reappear. The other girls' faces and need for friendly advice filled him with impatient disgust—why did they have to waste so much time? Why not leave Ariadne alone at the window? But there was to be no more Ariadne for the monster on that night.

On the following night excursions, the monster slowed his trips between the labyrinth and his mother's tower. He would try to steal a look at Ariadne. Sometimes he saw a girl strolling in the garden, or on the balconies that overlooked the garden, or in another window. But it was rarely her. When the monster did not see Ariadne, he could not rid himself of a lingering feeling of disappointment. However, when he did chance to see her now and then, the Minotaur felt a horrible, searing longing, followed by a painful sadness. Lovesickness was eating away at the monster once more. He wandered his dark underground halls between these visits conjuring images of Ariadne in his mind's eye, and dreaming—even though he told himself not to—of being next to her and accidentally knocking knees and feet together.

The monster considered sending a message to Ariadne and arranging a rendezvous in the palace gardens. He could, he reflected, send the message through his mother, who could use a trusted servant. They could see each other again. No more marriage proposals or dreams of idylls in the countryside together, but just the opportunity to be next to her again on a bench, nothing more. How could Ariadne begrudge the monster such a simple, heartfelt request? He would ask her for nothing, only for the small kindness of being near him and not hurting him.

However, the hideous ghost of Ariadne's laughter assailed the monster once more. Even if she were to meet him, and even if this rash meeting did not result in revealing the secret of his ability to move in and out of the labyrinth (a risk that started to make him uncomfortable), the monster saw a pitiable scene in his waking dream now: The two would meet in the gardens, under a bright moon. The moon's brightness would be harsh. It would reveal the monster in all his hideousness. Ariadne would approach with hesitant steps, curious but perhaps afraid. The unforgiving moon rays would show her the big bull's head blushing and staring down, the monster's big, thick, hairy fingers twisting nervously into each other, and she would laugh again at the silly picture of the oafish monster felled by puppy love.

IX. The Noble Hero Murders the Monster

WHILE THE MONSTER struggled with his melancholy longing for Ariadne, King Minos weaved the fateful web of events, which led to the Minotaur's death, exactly as the great goddess Aphrodite had promised.

The queen gave her son important news one evening on his visit:

You must be careful, dear child. There are now many men who wish to kill you. Men who are convinced you are a murderer and that your blood must be spilled in vengeance. You have become a true monster in the eyes of the world.

The monster was silent. This news hardly moved him: The great goddess had already assured the Minotaur that his fate was to be known as a great monster, whatever he did. Queen Pasiphae continued:

You do not understand. Everything is different now. You know how the Athenians have always made trouble for King Minos, how they never wanted to pay their taxes to Crete? Well, Minos has now devised a horrible punishment for them. Minos has said your bloodlust is unquenchable, and that you need to eat fresh victims. Can you believe this? You, my son, who have never eaten a morsel of meat, whose mouth salivates at fresh grass, you are now eating people alive according to my husband! So Minos has now decreed that the Athenians send seven virgin girls and seven young men. They are, supposedly, to be thrown into the labyrinth for you to feed upon.

No one has seen you in so long, except me. Now that you are hidden away, no one remembers your gentle soul. The tales they tell of the palace monster in his secret dungeon .... And now King Minos has decided that your notoriety—or your ability to rouse foreigners' nightmares—should be used to aid in tax collection ....

Promise me, please, that you will be careful. I know, just know, some hot-headed Athenian will enter the labyrinth aiming his axe at your neck.

Or better yet, run. Run away again. Go stow away on a ship bound for far distant lands. For the Red Sea coast. Or for India. But far, where no one can harm you.

The monster smiled and sighed at his mother's words. He showed no sign of worry and answered calmly:

I cannot run from myself. The gods will not lift my curse. I will be a monster everywhere I go. If not an Athenian, then it will be a Phoenician or Assyrian or Indian who will cut my throat.

Queen Pasiphae said no more. She looked at the wall, away from her son's monstrous animal face; her features were tense. She held the monster's hand ever more tightly. Despite his far larger size, the Minotaur felt her grip would crack the bones in his fingers.

That night, in his bed in the labyrinth, in that otherworldly still blackness, which made the existence of others feel like a strange hallucination to him, the monster mulled over his mother's words. King Minos's rash, vindictive actions would draw some would-be hero, he concluded. The prize was too tempting: The hideous underground monster, eater of virgin flesh, must be killed; the monster's hideous bull's head would make a fine trophy. His life thread would soon be cut.

The monster knew there was no escape. He reasoned that King Minos's horrible lies had doubtless skipped from one merchant's lips to another's throughout Greece, Egypt, Phoenicia, and all the other nearby lands. He would have to travel far indeed to find a place where the fame of the flesh-eating Minotaur had not spread. And even if there were such a place, what then? Would those strangers be somehow sympathetic to a monster with a bull's head? The monster knew his face alone would fill these strangers with terror, and he would, no doubt, be swiftly condemned as a curse by their foreign gods. I cannot escape myself, the monster thought over and over.

So, the monster's thoughts rolled on. Why not really become a monster? If he will be cut down sooner or later as a monstrous killer, if poets will sing for ages of his evil and cruel nature, why not make the lies into truth? The Minotaur had nothing to gain by living honorably; nobody would ever know or care. Why not knock some heads? It would be just to gore and beat the sycophantic snakes hissing and slithering through Knossos.

I could kill Ariadne, the monster thought. Beat that laughter into oblivion. The next time he saw her and her friends prancing in a window, he could walk over, climb in, reveal himself, and break their necks. It is not as if this behavior would hurt his marriage prospects. The monster summoned a mental picture of goring Ariadne's small body with his horns. None of it would change anything. Yes, I am free to do anything, the Minotaur thought—free because I am doomed.

Yet, he was not free. He forced himself to imagine hurting Ariadne. She would run. He would grab her arm; he would pull her shaking, screaming body towards him. She would beg for her life. There would be tears. Maybe she would mention a great love. Or a child inside her.

The monster knew he could not hurt her. He was not free, somehow, to be a monster. He could not make himself act the part, even in his imagination. The monster knew he would die, no matter what, but he could choose his manner of living. He chose to resist the gods' decree: The monster chose, at that moment, never to be a monster.

The monster that was not a monster soon had visitors to his underground apartments. The visits began with a girl screaming. Her screams, almost animal like, followed the monster everywhere he turned in the labyrinth. In between the screams, she called out desperate, begging prayers to gods who seemingly paid no attention. The Minotaur searched and searched through the hallways, but could not find her until one evening when he came home from a visit to his mother; he tripped over a girl's dead body. She was young and stiff and putrid. There was a blindfold bound tightly over her eyes and her wrists were tied behind her back; there was dried blood on those wrists from the rubbing of the raw, coarse ropes against her once soft skin. The dead girl's forehead had large gashes across it. It appeared to the Minotaur that the girl had died from a head wound.

The monster jumped back from the smell. He had never been near a dead body before and barely stopped himself from vomiting. He ran back to his suite of rooms.

The next evening the monster gently took the girl's dead body into the palace gardens and discreetly buried her behind the trees and bushes hiding the secret exit out of the labyrinth. He had found a coin lying on the ground nearby, and put it into her mouth as fare for the ferryman to take her across the River Styx into Hades.

Soon there were other screaming, bound prisoners wandering help-lessly through the labyrinth. When he heard them shouting, the Minotaur would try to find them. Usually he found only the dead bodies, and he would bury them in the night. The monster would place a coin in the corpse's mouth when he could find one.

Once the monster caught up with one of the poor bound prisoners. The monster touched the young boy tenderly and offered to help him es-cape. The boy cried for joy and offered many thanks until the monster re-moved the blindfold. Seeing himself face to face with the dreaded Minotaur, the boy scrambled and screamed, disappearing deep into the hallways of the labyrinth. The monster sighed, but decided he would still try to help the boy if he could.

He found the boy's corpse three days later—another long gash on the forehead. The monster dug the boy a small grave, but had no coin this time. He hoped that the ferryman would show pity and offer a free ride across the River Styx.

There was soon a new man in the labyrinth. He was tall, broad, and muscular. He was not blindfolded or bound. To the contrary, this man's free-swinging hands held an axe, and he kept a dagger tied to his waist. Tied to the dagger's sheath was an end of yarn connected to a distant ball of yarn back at the beginning of the labyrinth where he had entered. The great hero's secret helper held the other end of the yarn and had shown him the way to the Minotaur that night.

This man had not been sent to Knossos as a prisoner, to be dropped bound and blindfolded into the labyrinth. This was Theseus, prince and heir to the throne of Athens. He had reacted with rage to word of King Minos's decree that Athenian youths should be fed to the bloodthirsty Minotaur. He urged his father, the King of Athens, to raise a rebellion and declare Athens independent of Crete's overbearing dominion. The Athenian King, however, feared the might of Crete and judged his force no match for Minos. We must be patient, he counseled his son. Now is not the time.

Theseus could not bear the sight of his father or the quisling courtiers of the Athenian court, who feared Crete more than they loved Athens. Theseus let out his disgust at the world by hunting day and night in the countryside, and massacring deer, boars, birds, rodents, and any other living thing unfortunate enough to cross his path. Theseus could not spill enough blood to relieve his anguish at King Minos's decree to murder Athenian youth.

He slept in a royal hunting lodge with only a couple of trusted young grooms who cared for his hunting dogs and cleaned and skinned the carcasses. The hunting lodge was one large wooden room in a clearing in the forest, with narrow slits for windows and a small shrine to Artemis, goddess of the hunt. Given the ample supply of fresh meat from Theseus's axe, the little group in the hunting lodge ate nothing but barely roasted, rare animal flesh. Theseus, in fact, liked his meat barely cooked, so that the blood would still give it flavor.

Weeks passed this way in the hunting lodge. Theseus's father sent envoys to urge his son to return to his palace—the king needed his son's aid in governing Athens. One of these days, moreover, the king would die and Theseus would ascend to the throne. He must be up to speed on exactly what was happening in the city. Sulking in the woods and hacking deer was no way for a royal prince to learn how to shoulder his great responsibilities.

Theseus laughed at these pleas. He told each messenger to go away and to leave him alone. If words were not enough to secure Theseus's solitude, he would sick the pack of hunting dogs on the visitor, who would arrive back in Athens hobbling from vicious animal bites. Theseus had no thought for the future. He simply knew he could not bear to be near the Athenian royal court, and the killing of animals in the forest relieved his feelings of impotent fury.

While Theseus was ensconced at the hunting lodge, a strange new visitor came to Athens. She arrived on a merchant ship from Crete. She was taller than any woman in Athens and taller than almost every man, too. She had long, thick, straight blonde hair, which fell down half her back and sky blue eyes. Her hips curved ever so slightly below her waist, and she had full red lips. She wore a long, white linen dress, which fell to her ankles and covered her arms and most of her hands. All who saw her disembark found her to be both the most beautiful and the most intimidating woman they had ever seen.

The Cretan beauty wasted no time at the port, but hired a driver and wagon immediately and paid for passage to the royal palace at Athens. She approached the sentries at the gates and demanded entrance. She had a message for Prince Theseus, which was to be delivered to his ears alone. She would wait at the gates, if necessary, while her visit was announced.

After some delay, the woman was admitted to the palace. She was shown into a reception room where she was greeted by a jovial, rotund man, a counselor to the king. The counselor welcomed her to Athens and offered to convey her message to Theseus. He could also help advise the noble lady on finding a suitable inn, if she was looking for lodging, and perhaps could assist her in her other business on the Greek mainland.

My message is for Theseus alone. The message was told to me by the great goddess Aphrodite herself, and my instructions were to deliver the message directly to Theseus. Unless you wish to bring the goddess's terrible anger upon your city and your family, you should obey.

The woman stood very still and straight. Her head almost grazed the room's modest ceiling, and her cold eyes stared down at the short, plump older man. She said nothing more, but kept her gaze constantly upon him. The man looked down and fumbled for words. He started several sentences without being able to finish any of them. He felt hot and perspired everywhere; his clothes were soaking through. Beautiful as she was to look upon, the man felt he could not raise his head from the floor. Those blue eyes above were roasting him alive. Finally, he excused himself. The woman said nothing. She sat down on a couch in the corner of the room and waited.

The man scampered off to rustle up a priest of Aphrodite. This was not easy, as her cult was not fashionable in Athens at the time. Messengers were dispatched throughout Athens. With the help of a friendly foreign diplomat, the counselor was able to summon a visiting devotee of Aphrodite, a gentleman from Cyprus. The counselor thanked the Cypriot for offering to help and recounted his interview with the strange woman.

He sent the Cypriot into the room where the Cretan beauty waited patiently, motionless as a statue.

The counselor waited in the hallway. He paced back and forth. He tried to think about other things, but his mind could not shake the image of those searing eyes boring into his fat, sweaty flesh. He crept over to the door and tried to eavesdrop on the conversation, but he heard no sounds at all. Nonetheless, the Cypriot and the Cretan remained alone in the room for the balance of the afternoon. The Cypriot only emerged as daylight was fading.

The Cypriot exited by himself. The imposing giantess was still content to remain by herself. The Cypriot pulled the counselor aside by the elbow and hurriedly ushered him into a corner. The Cypriot was shaking. He spoke in a whisper:

She is the messenger of the great goddess Aphrodite. You must send her to Theseus at once. If you do not obey, the goddess's revenge upon you will be terrible.

The counselor's eyes were now bleary with sweat dripping from his forehead. He could not think clearly, but he knew he wanted this episode to end. These foreigners were leaving him ill at ease. With the cover of the priest's admonition, the counselor directed that a horse and wagon be prepared to escort the woman to Theseus's hunting lodge that very night. Anyway, the counselor reflected, Theseus probably will not listen to whatever this crazy woman says. Or his dogs will slice through her icy flesh and give her the whipping she deserves.

The woman nodded when she was told her wagon was ready. She walked through the palace corridors with her head high and erect, as if she were the queen of the Athenians, and it was only natural the palace would bend to her will. She mounted her seat in the wagon in one confident motion. The driver tried to make idle talk to pass the time—anecdotes about the recent good weather, how it was so nice to get to ride through the countryside, he usually only went back and forth between Athens and the port, and look at those stars. Could she make out constellations? He never learned how, but always thought that he should learn.

The woman said nothing. She stared straight ahead, over the head of the much shorter driver. The driver's chatter grew faster as he sought to fill the silence around him with something comforting to his ears. He was scared of this beautiful silent woman in the back seat. Something told him she would not hesitate to snap his neck if he fell out of her favor.

When they arrived at the hunting lodge, there was no light except an unusually bright full moon, which shattered the coverings of the branches and the foliage to light the wagon's way. The driver was alternately blinded and perplexed by the almost physically brutal, menacing moonlight. The woman did not seem to find anything unexpected in the pounding white light.

There was a circular clearing around the hunting lodge. The wagon stopped in this clearing in front of the door. There was a dull smoke coming from the chimney along with the smell of burning, dead animal flesh. Wait, the Cretan woman commanded the driver, and she stepped down without any assistance. The driver felt somehow bound to his seat by invisible ropes. He had trouble breathing. He looked down at his whip and mumbled words of reassurance to his horse.

The woman swung the door open and she strode right into the hunting lodge. Theseus and his two groomsmen were sitting in a corner nearby eating venison off of sticks and debating what to do with the now too large pile of deer hides in the lodge. She walked right up to Theseus and stared down at him.

Theseus did not flinch. He cocked his head up and grinned. Who are you? Did my father finally decide to send someone I would like? We could use more visitors like you.

I am the envoy of the great goddess Aphrodite. I have a message for you. Send the others away.

I like the sound of that, a beautiful woman with a message from the goddess of love. You are right, you and I should have some alone time. Gentlemen, why don't you go see if the lady's horse could use watering? We need some time alone for the special message from Aphrodite.

The groomsmen stood and walked out, snickering all the way and pointing to the Cretan beauty's different body parts. She paid no attention to them.

Once alone, Theseus asked the woman if she wanted to sit next to him on his frayed, aging couch, and maybe get out of that long heavy gown—

can't be comfortable, he said, in all this heat. Theseus himself had stripped to his undergarments.

This is the message for Theseus, Prince of Athens. The gods have fated you to be a great hero. You will travel to Knossos, and you will slay the Minotaur, the hideous monster in King Minos's labyrinth. You are to keep your mission silent. You shall bring suitable gifts with you to King Minos's court. You will be graciously received. There is a noble lady there, Ariadne, a ward and distant relation of the king. You must approach her alone for help in killing the monster. She will provide whatever assistance you may need.

Theseus looked at her. His arrogant eyes met her cold stare. He exploded in laughter.

Who put you up to this? Did one of my cousins dig you up at a brothel near the port? I must say, you are good. That almost convinced me. But can we end the theater? There are much more pleasant things for you here than pretending to be some holy oracle.

Watch your words, arrogant lord. Your impiety will not win you further favor from the gods. I am no whore. I am the messenger of the goddess, whom you are duty bound to obey.

I have come from Crete solely to discharge the obligation of providing your instructions from the goddess Aphrodite. I want nothing more to do with you or your disgusting appetites. My beauty is proof of the goddess's great power, and my beauty is for her alone to direct and use. In my childhood home, I spurned the love of a wretched little man, a cobbler's apprentice, who burned and deformed my face with a poisonous, burning liquid. I journeyed to the shrine of the great goddess Aphrodite, who took pity upon my sufferings. She remade me into this body, and saved me from the fate of being a deformed monster. Her one command was that I deliver this message to you at the appropriate time. I have obeyed and served the great goddess. I suggest you do the same.

The woman walked out of the hunting lodge without speaking further to Theseus. The two groomsmen looked surprised to see her so soon and so unruffled. She boarded the wagon and snapped her fingers. She was off. Theseus never saw her again.

The woman directed the wagon driver to take her directly back to the port, where she spent the night in a modest but respectable inn. She sailed home the next morning. The woman felt relieved that she had successfully fulfilled her bargain with the goddess. She laughed as she recalled the night when the Minotaur had spurned her offer of love and marriage on the high tree branches above the pilgrims' road.

Theseus left the hunting lodge for a walk that night in the nearby forest. The moon's bright rays lit his way, although he did not notice the strange nocturnal brightness. He brooded. He was not sure if the mad woman who had barged in on him was actually a messenger of the gods—though she certainly looked like an emissary of the goddess of beauty. But her idea was a good one. He was doing no good butchering the beasts of the forest. Sooner or later he was bound to kill some peasant's livestock by accident, anyhow, and stir up some unpleasant court case.

The next morning Theseus returned to Athens and ordered his servants to prepare for a journey to Knossos. His father, the king, was alarmed. Don't do anything rash, the king warned, we are not in a position to risk war with Crete. Don't worry, Theseus assured him, I am only going to learn the ways of the Cretan court. I want to make friends there, those who may be useful in the future. That is wise, agreed the king. Nevertheless, the king still sent a secret dispatch to his ambassador in Knossos with orders to watch Theseus closely and to intervene if needed.

Five days later, Theseus was received by King Minos at the palace in Knossos. Minos thanked the prince for the unexpected pleasure of his visit and ordered rooms to be made up in the palace for the visiting prince and his retinue. Theseus thanked King Minos for his gracious hospitality.

That night there was a banquet at the palace in Knossos in honor of the esteemed guest from Athens. Cretan society turned out in force to meet the dashing new visitor. Theseus wore a tight white cloak, which displayed his muscles clearly in their bulging girth; he liked to show off. Among the heads he turned that night was a petite young girl trying her best to sound worldly and clever. She was introduced to Theseus as the Lady Ariadne, a distant relation of some kind to King Minos. Theseus grinned at the name. He decided to test the goddess's strange message, so he allowed Ariadne to talk with him through the night. In Theseus's mind, Ariadne talked relentlessly about one boring thing after another—stupid gossip about which girl in the court was infatuated with which boy, the troubles she had with dressmakers, and how much better the food was when the cook was Phoenician. They were the best cooks she claimed. This Egyptian—ugh, King Minos and his love for everything Egyptian—made everything taste like a fried insect.

Theseus was bored with this talk. Usually he walked away from girls who would not shut up and who bored him so. But he was intrigued by the goddess's message, and he could not stop wondering whether this silly girl might be useful to him. He could always, he thought, discard her after the monster was cut down. He thought Ariadne was falling for him. This did not surprise Theseus in the least: He considered himself to be a remarkable specimen, and a prince to boot. He tossed in a word or two to hint that he found Ariadne fascinating and that her beauty was great. She tried to act as if these little compliments meant nothing, but with each one she leaned in closer, touched his hands, and involuntarily fixed and groomed her hair.

Theseus asked to speak to her later, alone. It was important, he said. Meet me in the palace gardens at midnight, Ariadne replied.

Between the banquet and the midnight meeting Ariadne ransacked her closet for the right dress and almost cried from her inability to locate that one right perfume bottle. It had the blue stopper, where could it be?

Theseus, on the other hand, napped. It was enervating to be stuck indoors with nothing to kill, and the girl's dull chatter had been exhausting.

Ariadne arrived in the gardens early. She paced around in a circle. She ran her fingers through her hair several times to make sure she had combed out all the knots; she considered her hair to be among her most attractive features and tonight it could not look like a tangled web on her head. She sniffed her wrists. The scent she had picked was perfect; the prince Theseus will swoon for me. But he needs to get here quickly. What if the scent wears off too soon?

Theseus lumbered into the garden rendezvous several minutes late. He stumbled into the unfamiliar surroundings and trampled a couple of flowerbeds under his feet. He apologized for being late. He said he had lost his way.

That is okay, Ariadne gushed. She wanted to appear mysterious, but her face would not cooperate. Red burst through her cheeks against her will.

Theseus looked at her and sighed. He walked over and grabbed her shoulders firmly. Ariadne felt a wave of excitement at his grip, even though it hurt a little. The fact that it hurt even made it a bit more exciting.

Listen, Theseus said. I came here on a secret mission. My mission is dangerous. I did not think I had time for anything else. But tonight, at dinner, I felt you and I were somehow connected. I feel that fates are linked. I usually have no patience with girls, but I could not pull away from you. You are so beautiful and charming. I want to be with you, but I can't unless you promise to help me, no matter what I might ask. You will need to leave Crete when we finish our work, but we will be together.

Yes, please, anything.

Are you sure? There is no turning back. Can I trust you?

Yes, of course, we are fated to be together.

I am here on a mission from the gods to slaughter the foul monster in the labyrinth, the Minotaur. I have my weapons, and I know that I can take him. He is just another smelly beast. Can you help me get in and out of the labyrinth?

Yes, I will, my love, I know where it is. And I know the trick of how to get in and out. One night, at a boring festival banquet, I got stuck sitting next to Daedalus, the little rodent man who built the labyrinth. He was desperate to impress me—you know how silly old men can be with pretty girls—and he told me how to navigate the labyrinth. You must tie a ball of string to a post at the beginning of one end and unwind as you go. Then you just follow the string back.

Good. Meet me in an hour. I will have my axe, bring the string. I do not want to waste any more time on this island.

Ariadne rushed back to her room in high spirits. She and Theseus were going to run away together. No more awkward dinner parties and scheming, judgmental girls in the palace. She would be Queen of Athens, and lie each night pressed against Theseus's big, hard body. Too bad about the Minotaur, she thought, he was sweet and harmless. But she supposed that sooner or later someone would come around to kill the monster. Nothing she could do about that. She had to look out for herself.

A little over an hour later Ariadne and Theseus stood at the entrance to the labyrinth. She handed him the ball of string while she held the other end. He grabbed her chin and angled her face up to his eyes. He kissed her briefly.

Had she ever seen the monster in all these years at the palace? Maybe before he was locked up?

No, Ariadne said she had never seen the beast.

Theseus entered the labyrinth. He did his best to creep stealthily, as he was a hunter and he did not want to alarm his prey. Despite these careful efforts, in the stillness of the labyrinth his steps echoed and reached the monster's sensitive ears.

The monster sat up and listened closely. He thought another of Minos's victims had been cast into the labyrinth. The monster was impressed by the courage of this one: no screams, no fright, just balanced, even steps in the hallways. The monster set out to find this new visitor and to offer his help.

The monster lit a lamp and went walking through the twisting halls, which he knew well by this time. He noticed as he walked closer to the steps, the steps seemed to grow louder and to be walking closer to him. Heartened by what he told himself was this good omen of steps finding steps, the monster quickened his pace.

The monster turned a sharp corner and there met the hero, Theseus. In fact, the two lightly bumped into each other before pulling apart. The monster held up his lantern and was surprised to see that this man had neither blindfold nor ropes. The monster stepped back when he saw the axe.

The frightened monster was no match for the decisive hero. Theseus quickly swung the heavy axe; the monster dropped the lamp and dived in the opposite direction, towards the floor, but the axe blade sliced most of the back of his right leg. The monster screamed in pain and could not get up.

Theseus walked over to the lamp and picked it up, afraid of an ambush in retaliation for his bold first move. He saw the monster helpless and whimpering on the ground. Theseus laughed, walked over slowly, and without any further fuss aimed and swung the axe, cleanly slicing the bull's head off of the human body. Theseus congratulated himself on a good straight stroke—all that practice on boars in the forest had done him well.

Thus the Minotaur died, with the sound of smug laughter ringing around him. His corpse was left to rot on the ground.

Theseus followed his string back to the labyrinth's entry. His secret helper, the eager Ariadne, was waiting loyally for him with the other end of the string. She kissed him passionately, although his lips barely responded. She did not fault him for his indifference; this must be how brave men acted after doing their daring deeds. Ariadne was sure now that she and her Athenian prince would sail off into happy ports and their love would be forevermore.

X. Epilogue: Alexandria, 200 B.C.E.

THE SCHOLAR REALIZED he had overdone it the night be-
fore. He had always had a sensitive stomach and he should have known that
the exotic food would wreak havoc with his fragile digestion. But the invi-
tation was too good to refuse: A great lord from far away India, reared on
legends of Alexander the Great's wars with King Porus of India, had traveled to pay homage to the tomb of the mighty Alexander. This Indian mag-
nate, apparently not trusting the quality of the local Greek cuisine (perhaps
an aversion to olives, the scholar wondered), had brought his own cook and
barrels of spices. Upon arriving in Alexandria, the visiting lord let it be
known there would be a great banquet at the villa he had rented.

The banquet was for important officials of the court and famous poets, not for the trudging infantry scholars who toiled away anonymously
each day in the Great Library. Nevertheless, this scholar had gotten lucky,
or so he thought: A friend with connections at the court finagled an invita-
tion for him. The scholar was awed by the glamorous company—men and
women in dazzling finery, an air thick with perfumes and spices and the
wine of Mareotis, and a long succession of speeches and musical performances and dances. Drunk on his own excitement, the scholar simply ate
whatever was placed in front of him, not caring to inquire what ingredients
made the foods so sharply fragrant and explosive on his tongue.

Back at his desk the next day at the Great Library, the scholar suffered
the consequences of his gluttony. His stomach contained a raging storm; he
felt liquids rise and fall and bubble and burst. Whenever the pain seemed to

recede, even slightly, a terrible stabbing sensation in his gut would double the poor scholar over. Fortunately, the scholar knew an excellent physician. He would see this good fellow later in the afternoon. The scholar was confident the physician would know the right draught to ease his suffering. Or, regardless, the pain would eventually go away of its own accord. After all, the scholar reflected, there were no recorded cases of lifelong stomach cramps. Or so the poor man hoped.

It was only a few hours until the afternoon appointment, but for now the scholar had come to the Great Library to distract himself with work. Yes, work would take his mind away from the pain in his belly. The scholar's task, for some months now, had been to compile and edit the legends surrounding King Minos of Crete. The Great Library's wise scholars would ultimately synthesize these disparate accounts and arrive at the proper and authoritative narrative of the ancient king's reign.

That day's task was a manuscript from Rhodes. The manuscript had been given to an Alexandrian merchant by a relation in Rhodes on his last voyage to the island. Having no use for the old scroll, the Alexandrian merchant graciously donated it to the Great Library, where it had become the scholar's burden to decipher and edit.

Beating back the pain in his stomach, the scholar started to read:

King Minos angered the god Poseidon by refusing to fulfill his promise to sacrifice a great white bull.

Something is missing, the scholar noted: Why would Minos have promised to sacrifice a bull? Why renege on the promise? And what difference would the color of the hide make? Bulls are valued for the quality of their meat and the scent of their burning fat. This all seemed unsatisfactory, but it was roughly consistent with several other manuscripts. Another rising wave of hot liquid in the stomach. His upper chest burned. Ignore it, the scholar thought, time to read on:

To punish King Minos, the great god Poseidon afflicted Queen Pasiphae with a consuming lust for the white bull. Pasiphae had the master craftsman Daedalus build for her an elaborate wooden disguise, so that she would appear as a cow. So disguised, Pasiphae lay with the bull, which was easily duped into thinking she was one of its own kind. Such was the skill of Daedalus's craft.

The scholar tried to imagine the scene in his mind: Pasiphae in a garishly painted wooden contraption pretending to be a cow and trying desperately to seduce the bull. The thought made the scholar laugh hard—which then aggravated his stomach pain, causing the poor man to lurch to the side of the bench in pain. He sat up again, determined to stay serious, if only for his gastrointestinal peace.

The scholar made a new note: Consider whether this legend is a satirical tale designed to undermine King Minos by laughing at his wife's ridiculous behavior and abnormal sexual appetites. Potential hypothesis to consider: The legend of Pasiphae and the bull was pornographic propaganda spread by the king's enemies.

The scholar continued:

Queen Pasiphae became pregnant by the bull. Her child was the Minotaur, a hideous monster with the body of a man and the head of a bull. The Minotaur ate only human flesh. To protect the people of Crete from the monster's feeding and killing, King Minos directed Daedalus to design and construct a great labyrinth underneath the palace to imprison the Minotaur.

This was better, the scholar thought. Minos was punished for his disobedience to the gods by being afflicted with a monster in his home. Good lesson and moral there. This tale may prove useful. The description of the monster will hold the attention of the schoolboys who really need to learn the importance of piety. Yes, there may be something of pedagogical value. But we will need to find a way to get rid of the silly pornographic part.

The text continued:

Minos had been angered by the Athenians. His son had been a great wrestler and had won a competition at Athens. The Athenians, in their fury, had murdered Minos's son. So Minos punished them by demanding they send seven virgin girls and seven young men each year to Knossos to be sent into the labyrinth as food for the Minotaur.

Yet again, the scholar sighed, the manuscript disappoints. It is utterly absurd to believe King Minos would have let his son, a royal prince, wrestle naked in front of a great crowd, much less chance a humiliating defeat at the hands of some lout from the countryside. No, this made no sense. The scholar deduced that the wrestler's story was a late interpolation to provide some explanation as to why Minos was angry at the Athenians. The original legend must have skipped that detail.

The scholar read on:

Brave and noble Theseus, son of the King of Athens, determined to put an end to the Minotaur's killing. He volunteered to be one of the seven young men. His father begged him not to go, but Theseus insisted. Theseus arrived in Knossos with his thirteen companions. The night before they were to be led down to the labyrinth, the Athenians dined with King Minos and his family. At this banquet Minos's daughter Ariadne fell in love with the mighty hero, Theseus.

Whoever wrote this scroll was an ignorant fool, the scholar thought. Why would Minos have invited his victims to dinner? So he could pity them? Or gloat over them? Again, this seemed to him to be a late interpolation, a flimsy plot device to get Theseus and Ariadne to meet. At least the scholar's stomach was feeling a little better.

The tale continued:

Ariadne could not bear the thought of Theseus dying in the labyrinth. She gave him a ball of string to unravel as he went into the labyrinth. He could follow the string to find his way back. Theseus thanked the princess, took the string, and promised to sail away with her and to marry her after he slayed the Minotaur. Theseus entered the labyrinth, found the Minotaur, killed the monster with his bare hands, and used the string to find his way out. Theseus, Ariadne, and the other Athenians escaped Crete by cover of night. Theseus abandoned Ariadne on the island of—the writing was illegible here, someone back in Rhodes had obviously spilled some sauce or wine on that part of the scroll. The legible text picks up with—Ariadne was inconsolable in her great grief . . .

Ouch—terrible, sharp stabbing pains right in the back of the scholar's stomach. He was not going to get more work done. Best to see if the doctor could see him earlier.

And what good was this manuscript? Not only was it full of implausible plot devices and disgusting pornography, but it also had the noble hero abandoning the beautiful princess, who had risked everything to help him and who had believed his promises of love and marriage. Dumping princesses on the first available rock in the sea was no way for a hero to behave. What a wretched story all around. The scholar could not wait to be promoted to more interesting work.

CPSIA information can be obtained at www.ICGtesting.com
Printed in the USA
LVOW11*1801231215

467350LV00002B/6/P